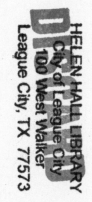

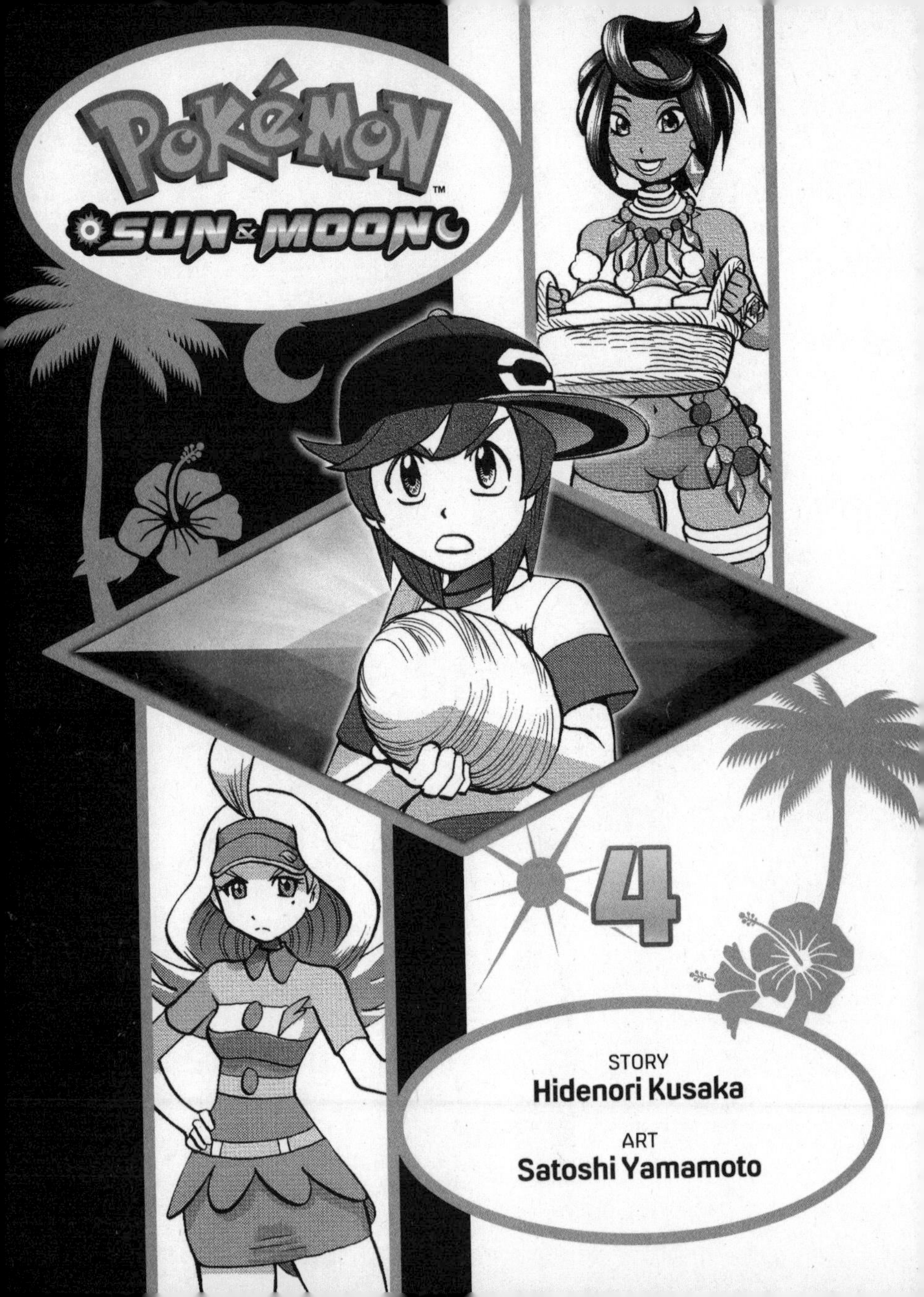

Pokémon™ Sun & Moon

4

STORY
Hidenori Kusaka

ART
Satoshi Yamamoto

Introduction

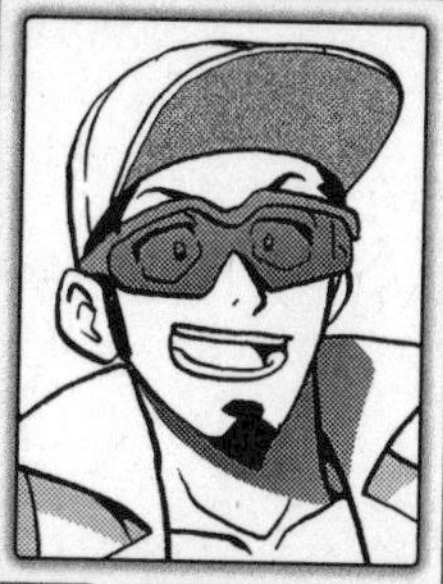

Professor Kukui

A Pokémon researcher with a laboratory on Melemele Island. An expert on Pokémon moves who likes to experience these Pokémon moves used against himself!

Moon

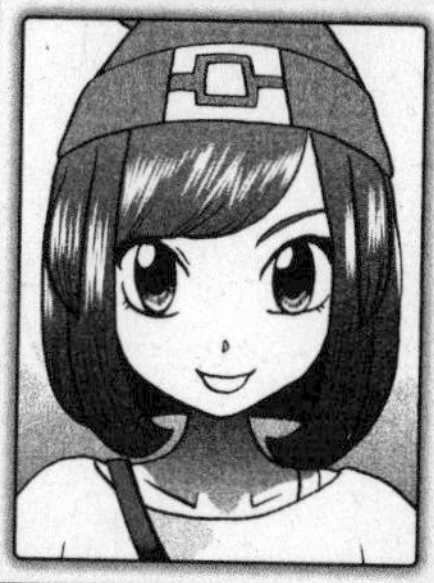

Another of the main characters of this tale. A pharmacist who has traveled to Alola from a faraway region. She is a self-confident, original thinker. She is also an excellent archer.

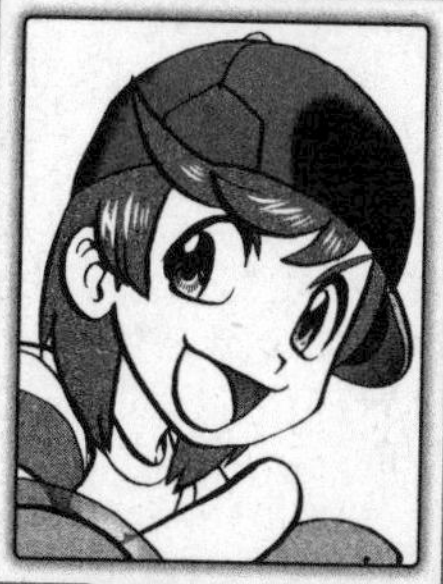

Sun

One of the main characters of this tale. A young Pokémon Trainer who makes a living doing all sorts of odd jobs, including working as a delivery boy. His dream is to save up a million dollars!

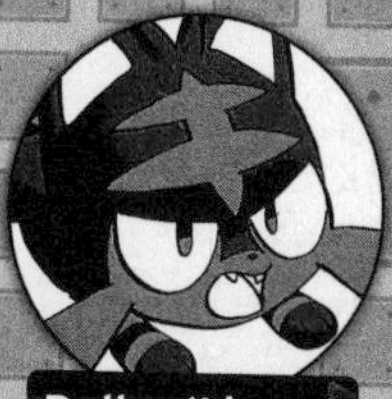

Dollar (Litten)

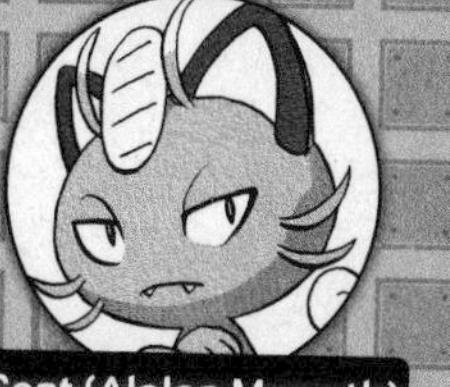

Cent (Alolan Meowth)

The Story Thus Far...

The Alola region consists of numerous tropical islands. Moon, a pharmacist from another region, comes to this flower-filled vacation paradise on an important errand. On one of Alola's pristine beaches, she meets a boy named Sun. Sun works various odd jobs in addition to the delivery service he runs in order to reach his goal of saving up a million dollars. Moon doesn't understand why he would want so much money, but they become friends and travel to Professor Kukui's laboratory together. Meanwhile, at Iki Town on Melemele Island, preparations are in full swing for the Full Power Festival...

Character

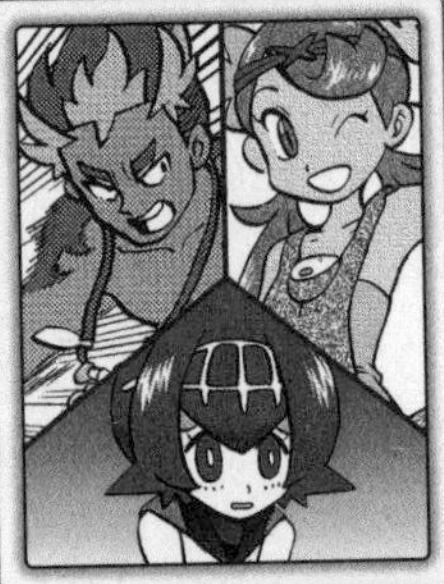

Kiawe, Mallow, Lana

Skilled Trainers and the Trial Captains of Akala Island.

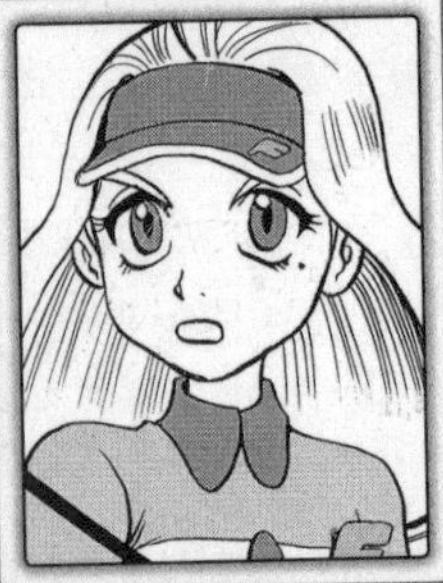

Kahili

A professional golfer who travels all over the world. She has been summoned home to Alola by Hala because it seems a catastrophe is about to befall the region.

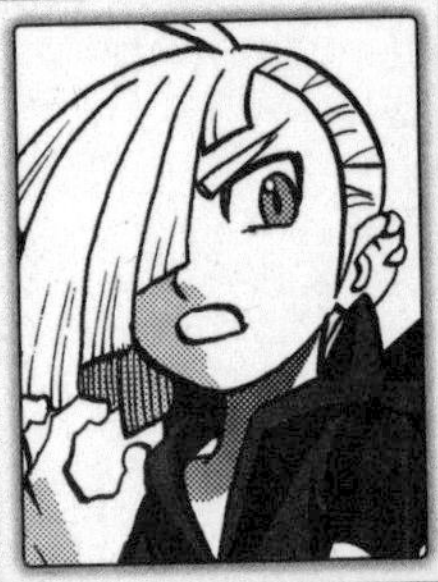

Gladion

A loner with a mysterious Pokémon named Type: Null. Why is he so interested in a mysterious rift in the sky...?

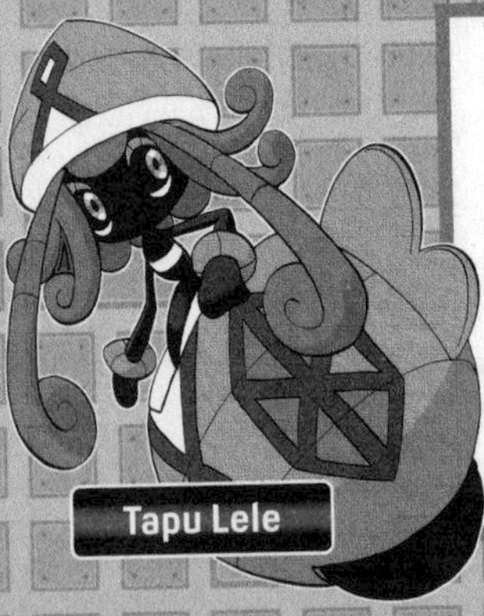

Tapu Lele

Each of the four islands of Alola have a guardian called a Tapu. Recently, the Tapu have become agitated... The island leaders use the festival's Pokémon tournament to choose a champion to get to the root of the problem and soothe the Tapu.

Sun wins the tournament, but now he must prove his mettle to the three trial captains: Kiawe, Lana and Mallow. Only then will he be permitted to embark on the Island Challenge to meet the four Tapu, present them with a rare berry and learn more about the crisis facing Alola.

Meanwhile, Moon heads to Lush Jungle with Mallow to acquire the mysterious unnamed berry for Sun. En route, they observe Tapu Lele battling a mysterious creature emerging from a rift in the sky... Then, with the help of Mallow's Pokémon, Moon manages to find the berry!

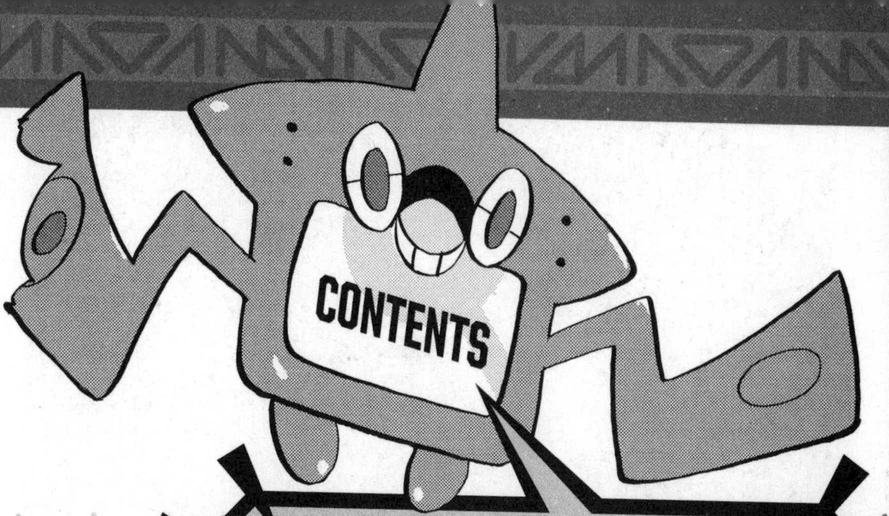

CONTENTS

Zzt zzt...♫

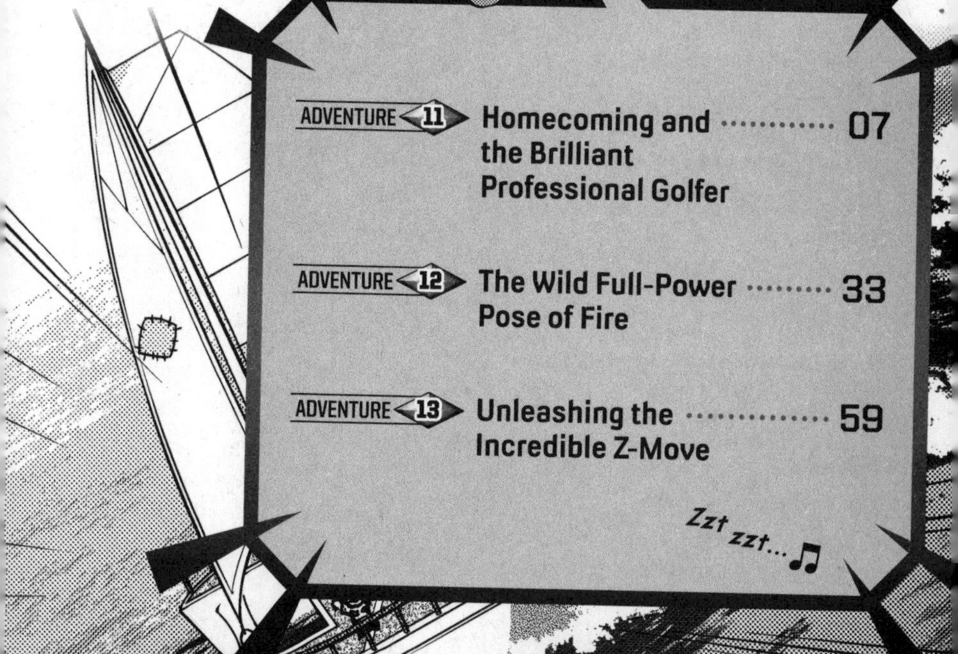

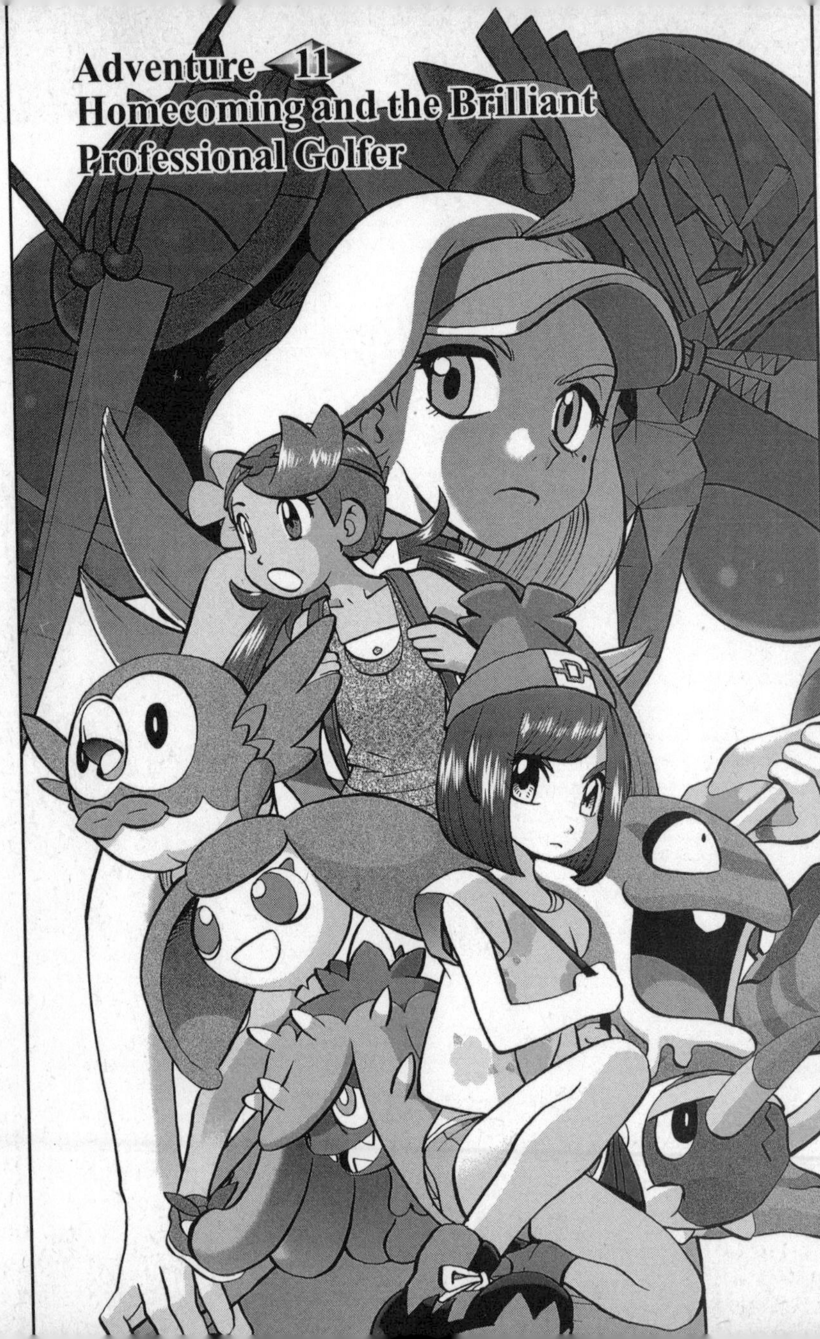
Adventure 11
Homecoming and the Brilliant Professional Golfer

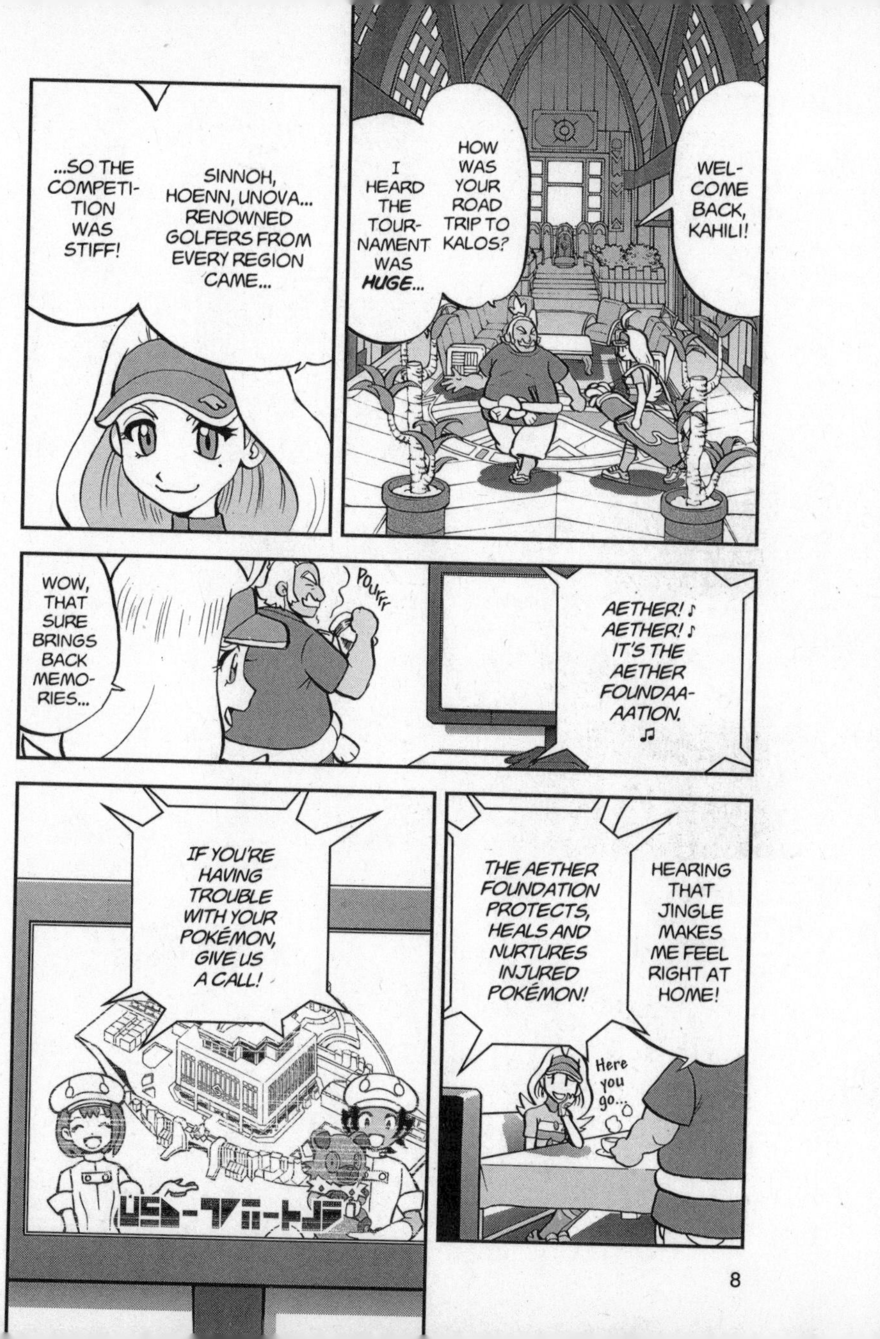
WELCOME BACK, KAHILI!
HOW WAS YOUR ROAD TRIP TO KALOS?
I HEARD THE TOURNAMENT WAS HUGE...
SINNOH, HOENN, UNOVA... RENOWNED GOLFERS FROM EVERY REGION CAME...
...SO THE COMPETITION WAS STIFF!
AETHER! ♪ AETHER! ♪ IT'S THE AETHER FOUNDAAAATION. ♫
Poukrr
WOW, THAT SURE BRINGS BACK MEMORIES...
HEARING THAT JINGLE MAKES ME FEEL RIGHT AT HOME!
THE AETHER FOUNDATION PROTECTS, HEALS AND NURTURES INJURED POKÉMON!
Here you go...
IF YOU'RE HAVING TROUBLE WITH YOUR POKÉMON, GIVE US A CALL!

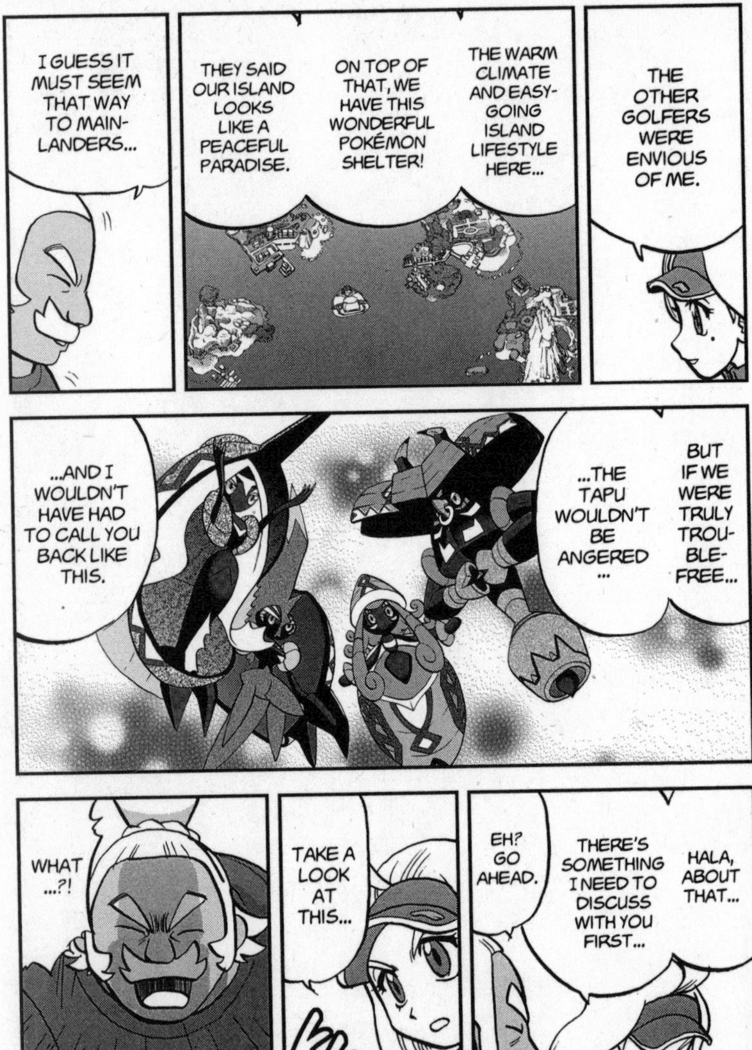
THE OTHER GOLFERS WERE ENVIOUS OF ME.
THEY SAID OUR ISLAND LOOKS LIKE A PEACEFUL PARADISE.
ON TOP OF THAT, WE HAVE THIS WONDERFUL POKÉMON SHELTER!
THE WARM CLIMATE AND EASY-GOING ISLAND LIFESTYLE HERE...
I GUESS IT MUST SEEM THAT WAY TO MAIN-LANDERS...
BUT IF WE WERE TRULY TROUBLE-FREE...
...THE TAPU WOULDN'T BE ANGERED ...
...AND I WOULDN'T HAVE HAD TO CALL YOU BACK LIKE THIS.
HALA, ABOUT THAT...
THERE'S SOMETHING I NEED TO DISCUSS WITH YOU FIRST...
EH? GO AHEAD.
TAKE A LOOK AT THIS...
KLTTR
WHAT ...?!

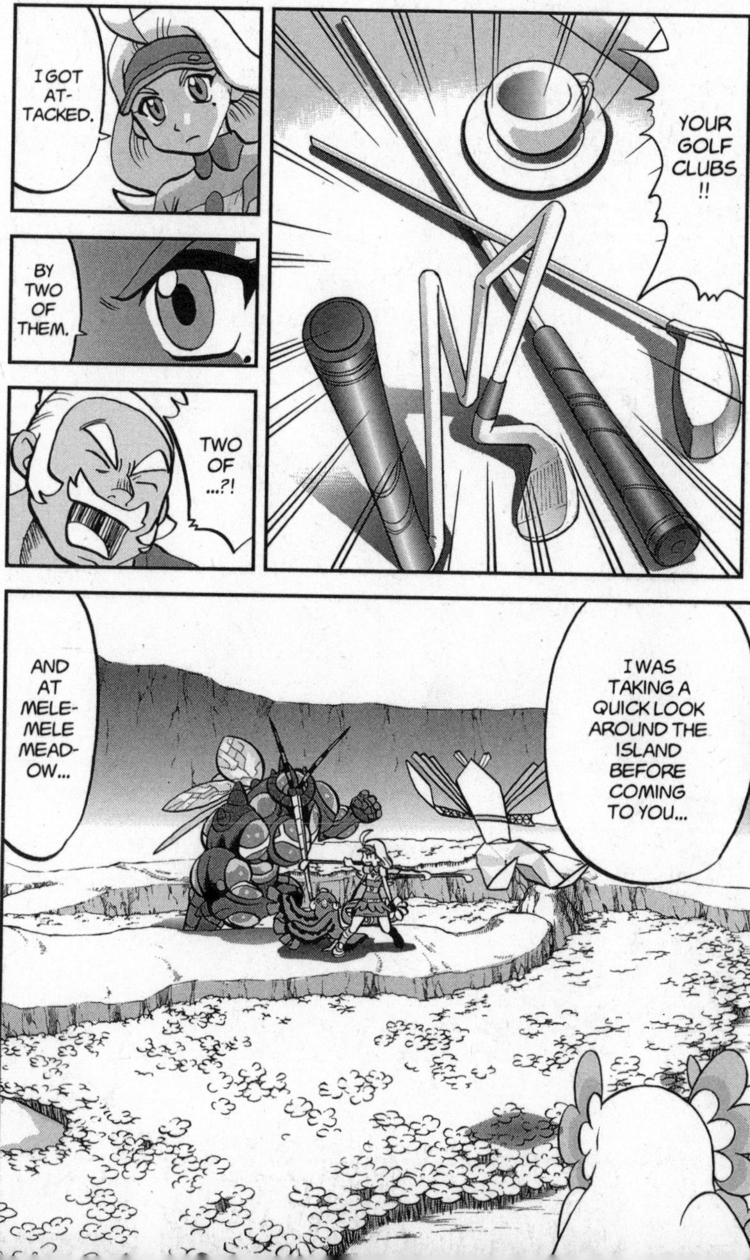
YOUR GOLF CLUBS !!
I GOT AT- TACKED.
BY TWO OF THEM.
TWO OF ...?!
I WAS TAKING A QUICK LOOK AROUND THE ISLAND BEFORE COMING TO YOU...
AND AT MELE- MELE MEAD- OW...

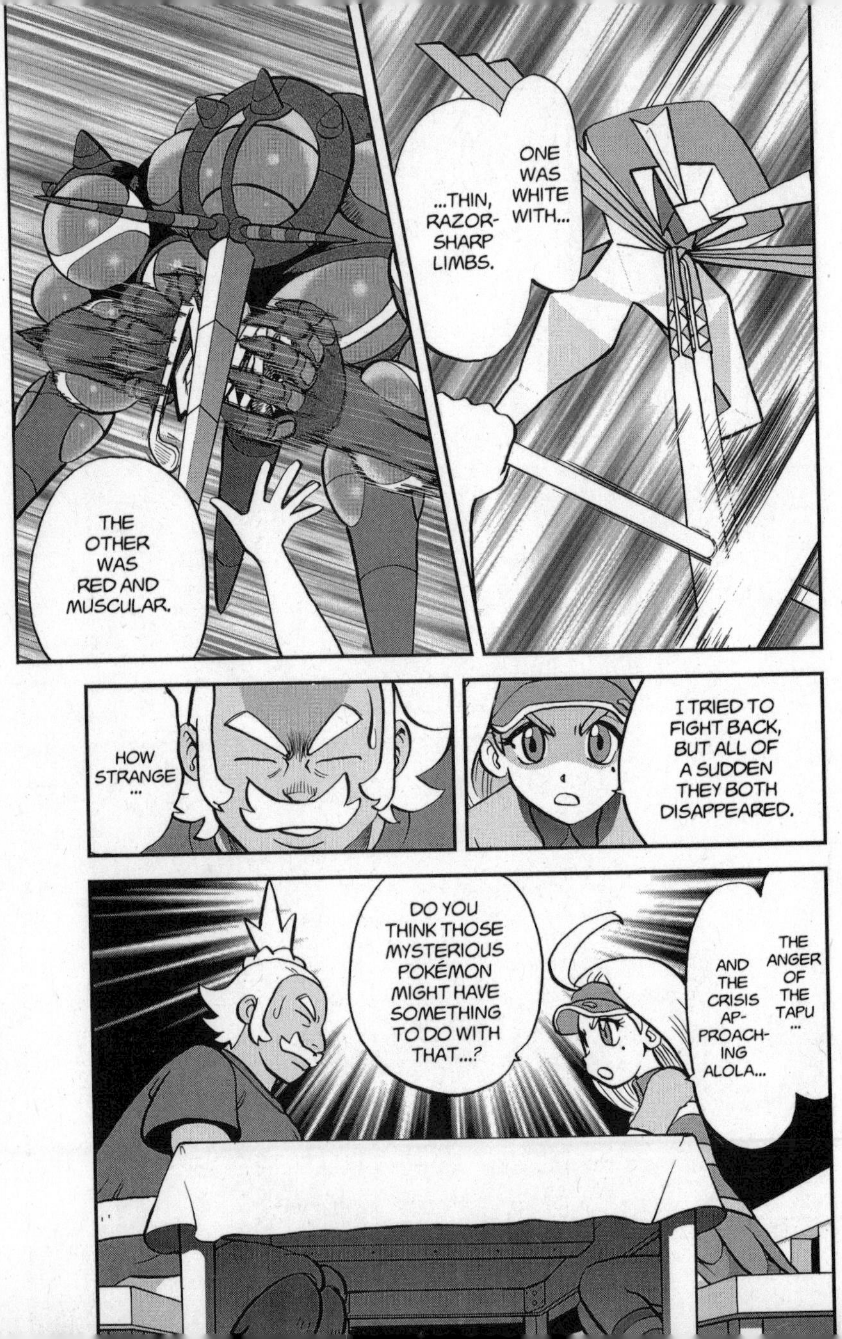
ONE WAS WHITE WITH...
...THIN, RAZOR-SHARP LIMBS.
THE OTHER WAS RED AND MUSCULAR.
I TRIED TO FIGHT BACK, BUT ALL OF A SUDDEN THEY BOTH DISAPPEARED.
HOW STRANGE ...
THE ANGER OF THE TAPU ...
AND THE CRISIS AP-PROACH-ING ALOLA...
DO YOU THINK THOSE MYSTERIOUS POKÉMON MIGHT HAVE SOMETHING TO DO WITH THAT...?

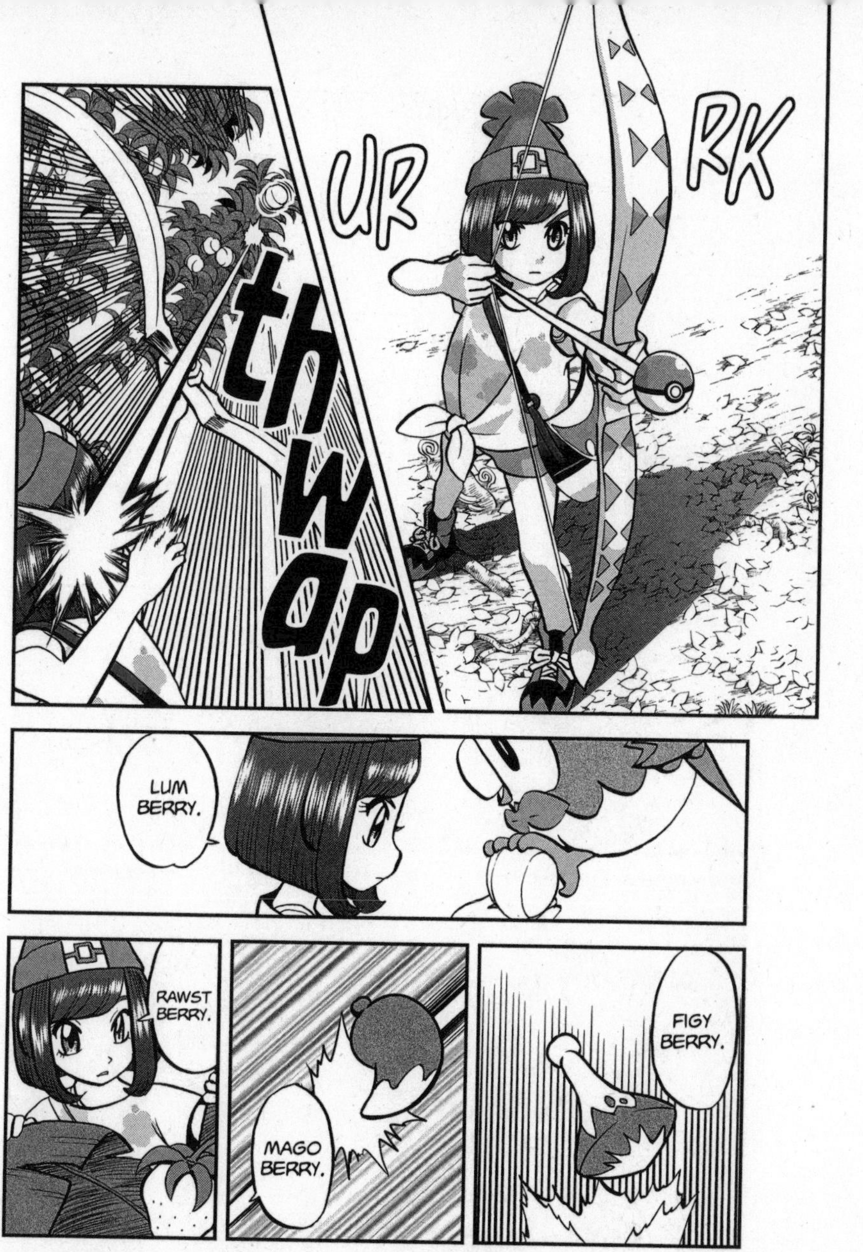
UR RK
thwap
LUM BERRY.
FIGY BERRY.
MAGO BERRY.
RAWST BERRY.

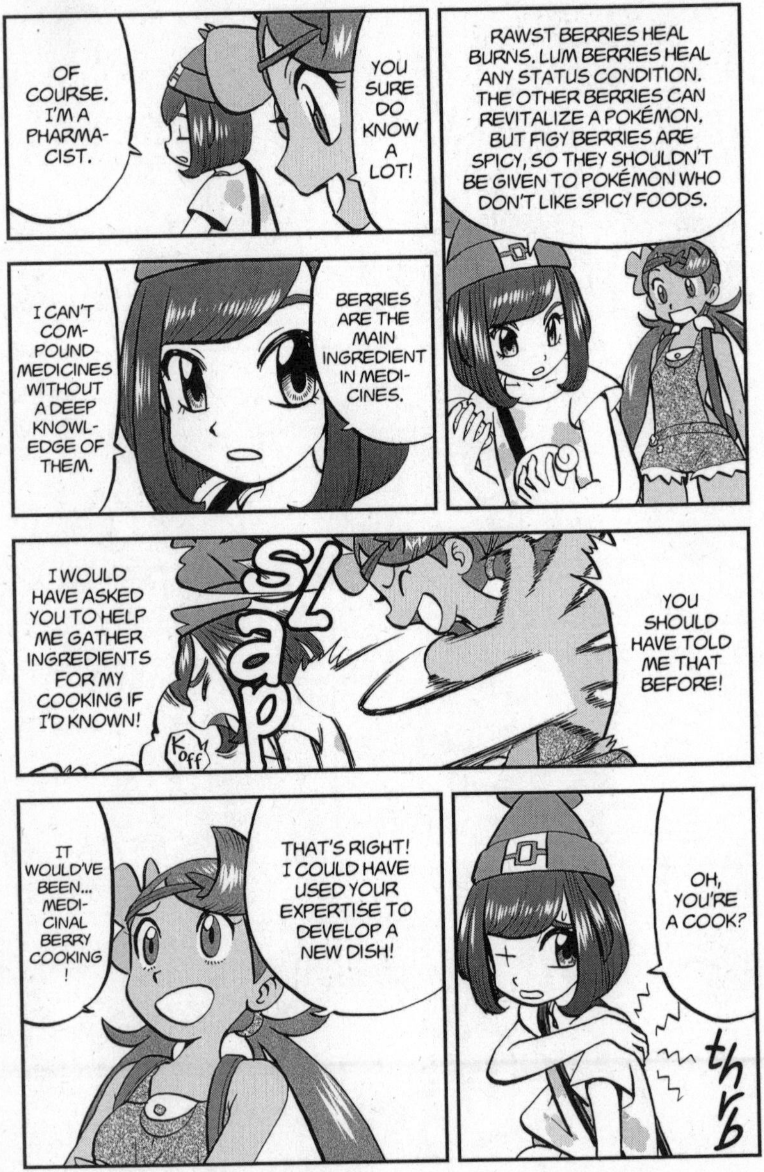
RAWST BERRIES HEAL BURNS. LUM BERRIES HEAL ANY STATUS CONDITION. THE OTHER BERRIES CAN REVITALIZE A POKÉMON. BUT FIGY BERRIES ARE SPICY, SO THEY SHOULDN'T BE GIVEN TO POKÉMON WHO DON'T LIKE SPICY FOODS.
YOU SURE DO KNOW A LOT!
OF COURSE. I'M A PHARMA-CIST.
BERRIES ARE THE MAIN INGREDIENT IN MEDI-CINES.
I CAN'T COM-POUND MEDICINES WITHOUT A DEEP KNOWL-EDGE OF THEM.
YOU SHOULD HAVE TOLD ME THAT BEFORE!
SLAP
I WOULD HAVE ASKED YOU TO HELP ME GATHER INGREDIENTS FOR MY COOKING IF I'D KNOWN!
Koff
OH, YOU'RE A COOK?
thrb
THAT'S RIGHT! I COULD HAVE USED YOUR EXPERTISE TO DEVELOP A NEW DISH!
IT WOULD'VE BEEN... MEDI-CINAL BERRY COOKING!

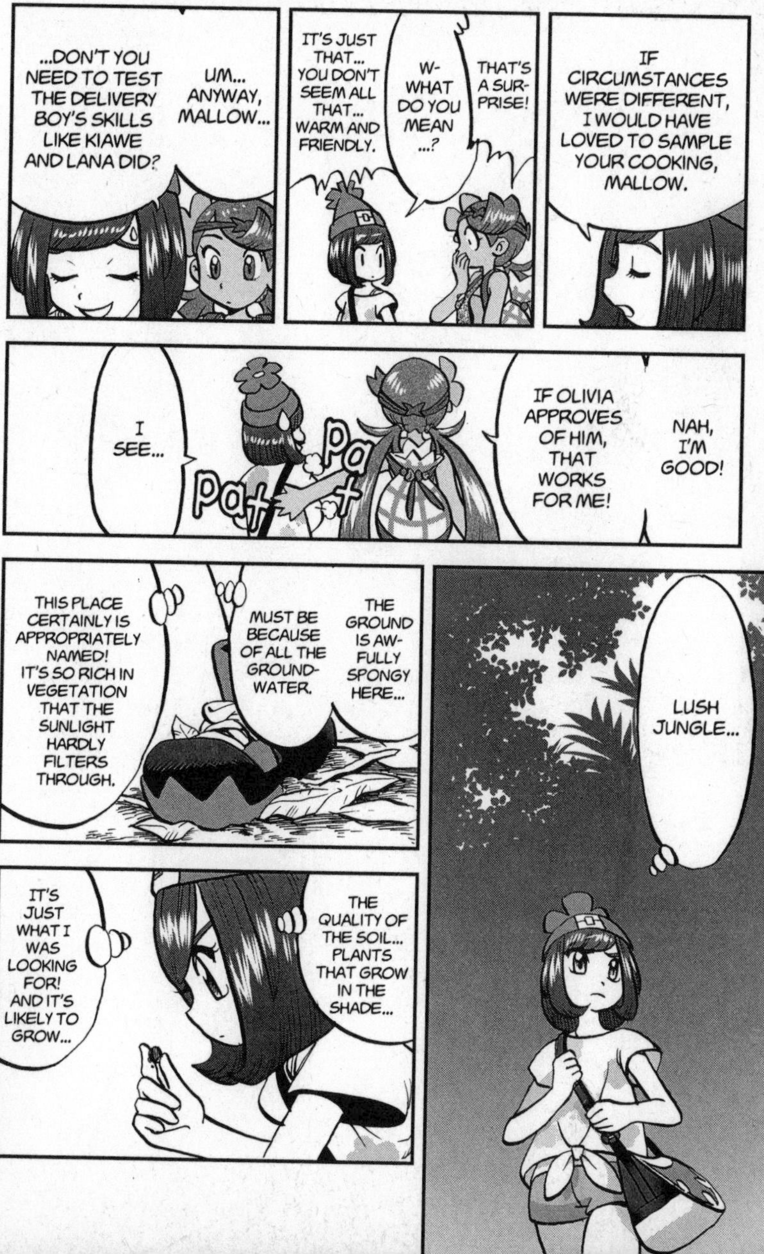
IF CIRCUMSTANCES WERE DIFFERENT, I WOULD HAVE LOVED TO SAMPLE YOUR COOKING, MALLOW.
THAT'S A SUR-PRISE!
W-WHAT DO YOU MEAN ...?
IT'S JUST THAT... YOU DON'T SEEM ALL THAT... WARM AND FRIENDLY.
UM... ANYWAY, MALLOW...
...DON'T YOU NEED TO TEST THE DELIVERY BOY'S SKILLS LIKE KIAWE AND LANA DID?
NAH, I'M GOOD!
IF OLIVIA APPROVES OF HIM, THAT WORKS FOR ME!
pat pat
I SEE...
LUSH JUNGLE...
THE GROUND IS AW-FULLY SPONGY HERE...
MUST BE BECAUSE OF ALL THE GROUND-WATER.
THIS PLACE CERTAINLY IS APPROPRIATELY NAMED! IT'S SO RICH IN VEGETATION THAT THE SUNLIGHT HARDLY FILTERS THROUGH.
THE QUALITY OF THE SOIL... PLANTS THAT GROW IN THE SHADE...
IT'S JUST WHAT I WAS LOOKING FOR! AND IT'S LIKELY TO GROW...

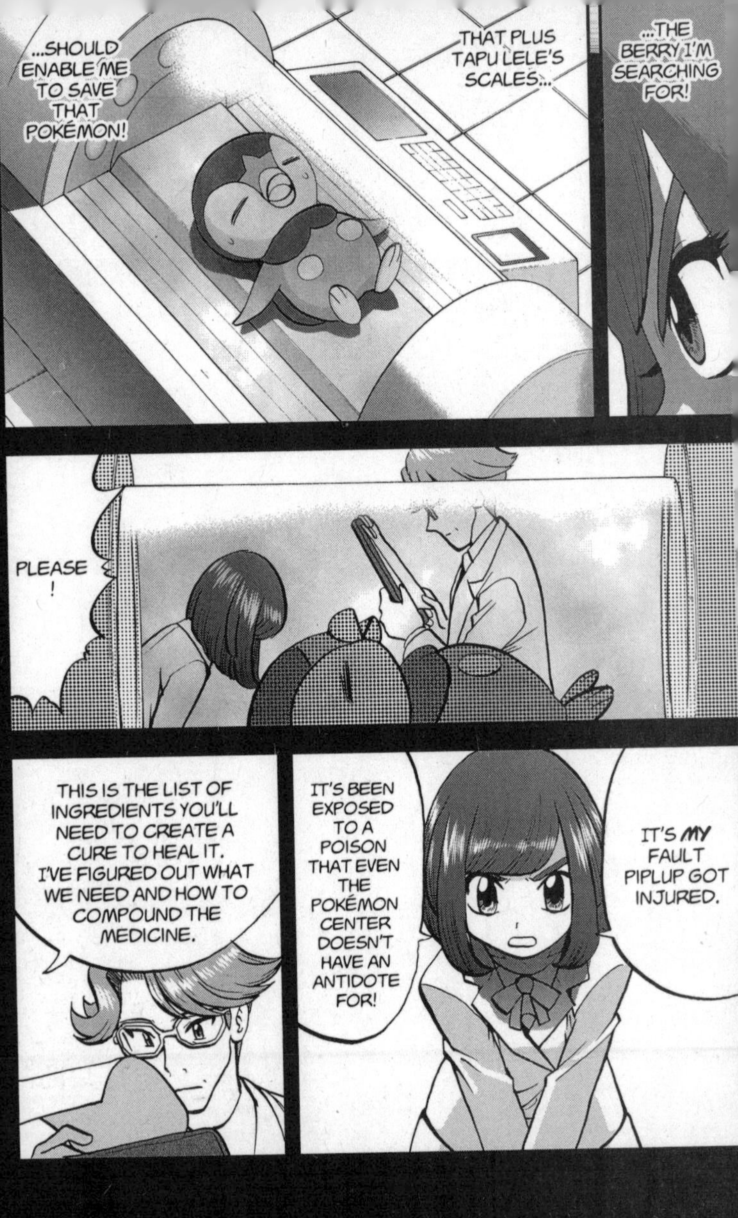
...THE BERRY I'M SEARCHING FOR!
THAT PLUS TAPU LELE'S SCALES...
...SHOULD ENABLE ME TO SAVE THAT POKÉMON!
PLEASE!
IT'S MY FAULT PIPLUP GOT INJURED.
IT'S BEEN EXPOSED TO A POISON THAT EVEN THE POKÉMON CENTER DOESN'T HAVE AN ANTIDOTE FOR!
THIS IS THE LIST OF INGREDIENTS YOU'LL NEED TO CREATE A CURE TO HEAL IT. I'VE FIGURED OUT WHAT WE NEED AND HOW TO COMPOUND THE MEDICINE.

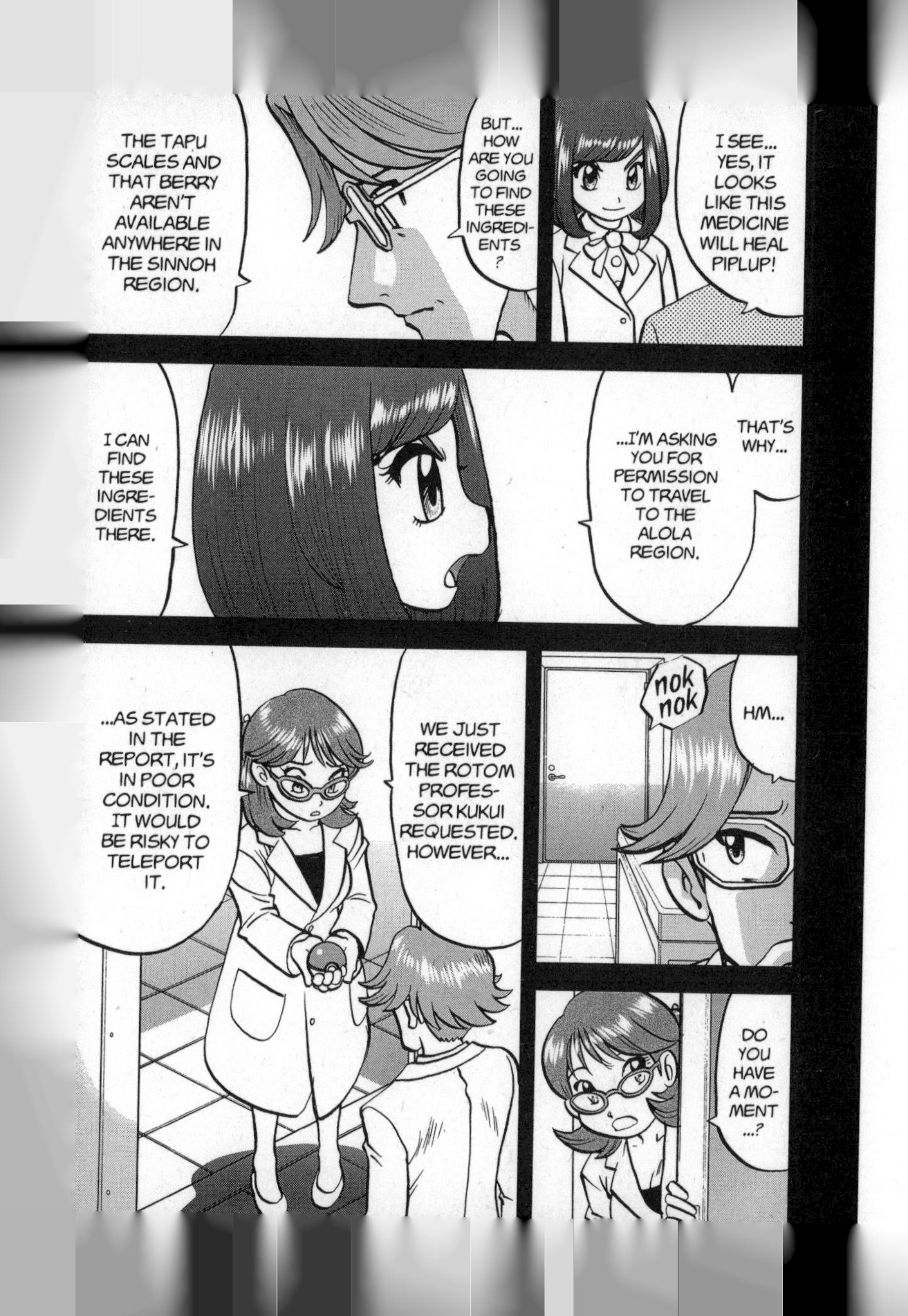
I SEE... YES, IT LOOKS LIKE THIS MEDICINE WILL HEAL PIPLUP!
BUT... HOW ARE YOU GOING TO FIND THESE INGREDIENTS?
THE TAPU SCALES AND THAT BERRY AREN'T AVAILABLE ANYWHERE IN THE SINNOH REGION.
THAT'S WHY...
...I'M ASKING YOU FOR PERMISSION TO TRAVEL TO THE ALOLA REGION.
I CAN FIND THESE INGREDIENTS THERE.
HM...
nok nok
DO YOU HAVE A MOMENT...?
WE JUST RECEIVED THE ROTOM PROFESSOR KUKUI REQUESTED. HOWEVER...
...AS STATED IN THE REPORT, IT'S IN POOR CONDITION. IT WOULD BE RISKY TO TELEPORT IT.

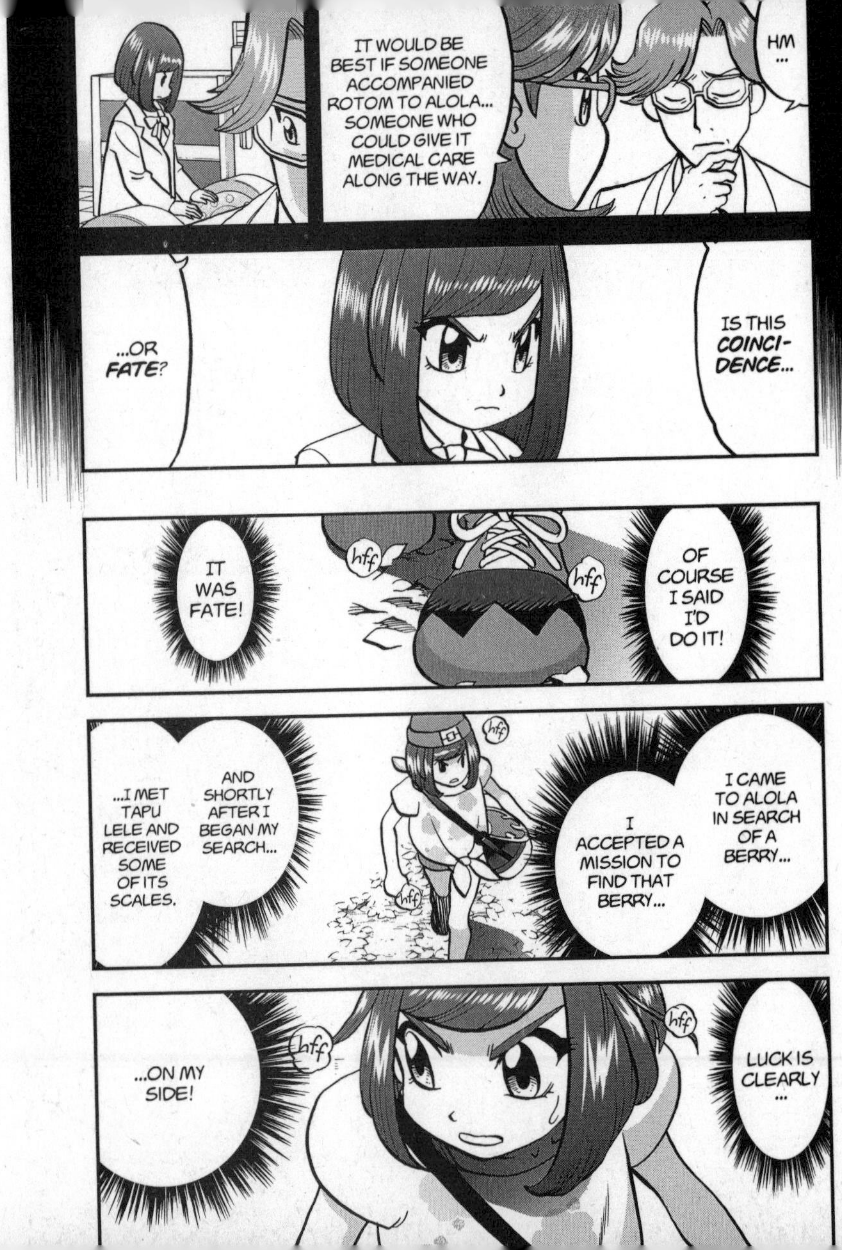
HM ...
IT WOULD BE BEST IF SOMEONE ACCOMPANIED ROTOM TO ALOLA... SOMEONE WHO COULD GIVE IT MEDICAL CARE ALONG THE WAY.
IS THIS *COINCIDENCE*...
...OR *FATE*?
OF COURSE I SAID I'D DO IT!
hff
hff
IT WAS FATE!
hff
I CAME TO ALOLA IN SEARCH OF A BERRY...
I ACCEPTED A MISSION TO FIND THAT BERRY...
hff
AND SHORTLY AFTER I BEGAN MY SEARCH...
...I MET TAPU LELE AND RECEIVED SOME OF ITS SCALES.
LUCK IS CLEARLY ...
hff
hff
...ON MY SIDE!

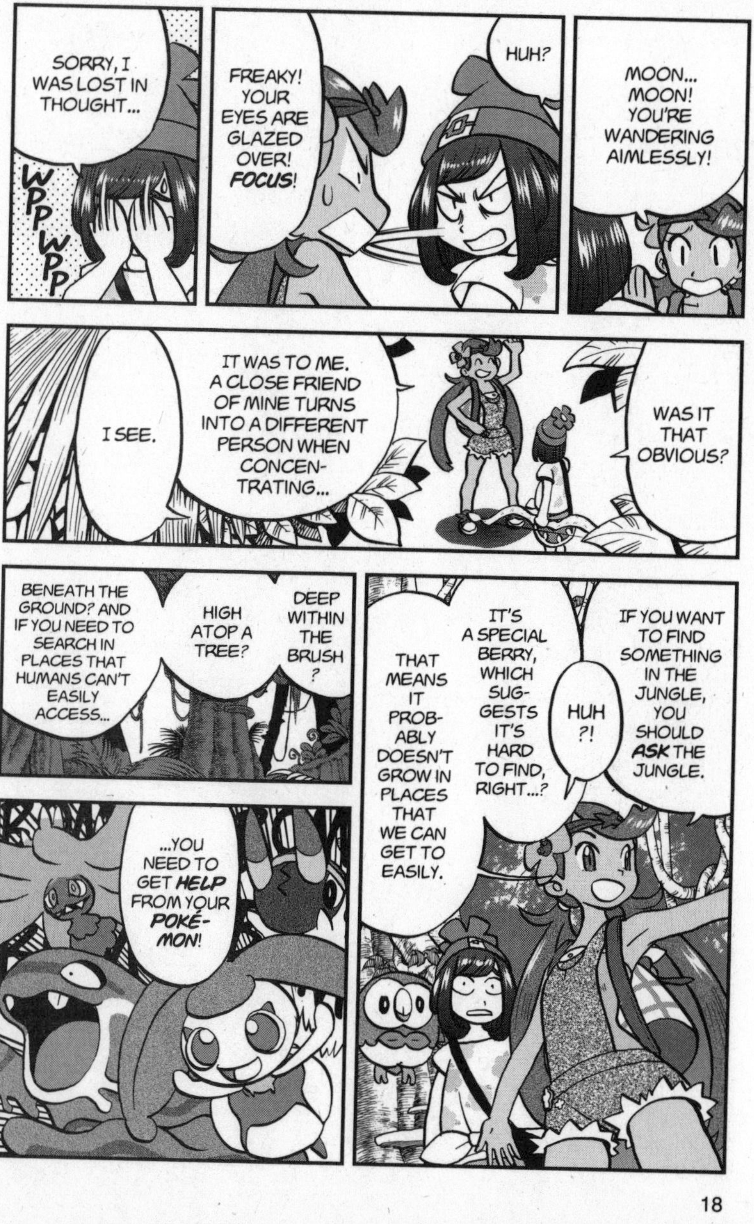
MOON... MOON! YOU'RE WANDERING AIMLESSLY!
HUH?
FREAKY! YOUR EYES ARE GLAZED OVER! **FOCUS**!
SORRY, I WAS LOST IN THOUGHT...
WPP WPP
WAS IT THAT OBVIOUS?
IT WAS TO ME. A CLOSE FRIEND OF MINE TURNS INTO A DIFFERENT PERSON WHEN CONCEN-TRATING...
I SEE.
IF YOU WANT TO FIND SOMETHING IN THE JUNGLE, YOU SHOULD **ASK** THE JUNGLE.
HUH?!
IT'S A SPECIAL BERRY, WHICH SUG-GESTS IT'S HARD TO FIND, RIGHT...?
THAT MEANS IT PROB-ABLY DOESN'T GROW IN PLACES THAT WE CAN GET TO EASILY.
DEEP WITHIN THE BRUSH?
HIGH ATOP A TREE?
BENEATH THE GROUND? AND IF YOU NEED TO SEARCH IN PLACES THAT HUMANS CAN'T EASILY ACCESS...
...YOU NEED TO GET **HELP** FROM YOUR **POKÉ-MON**!

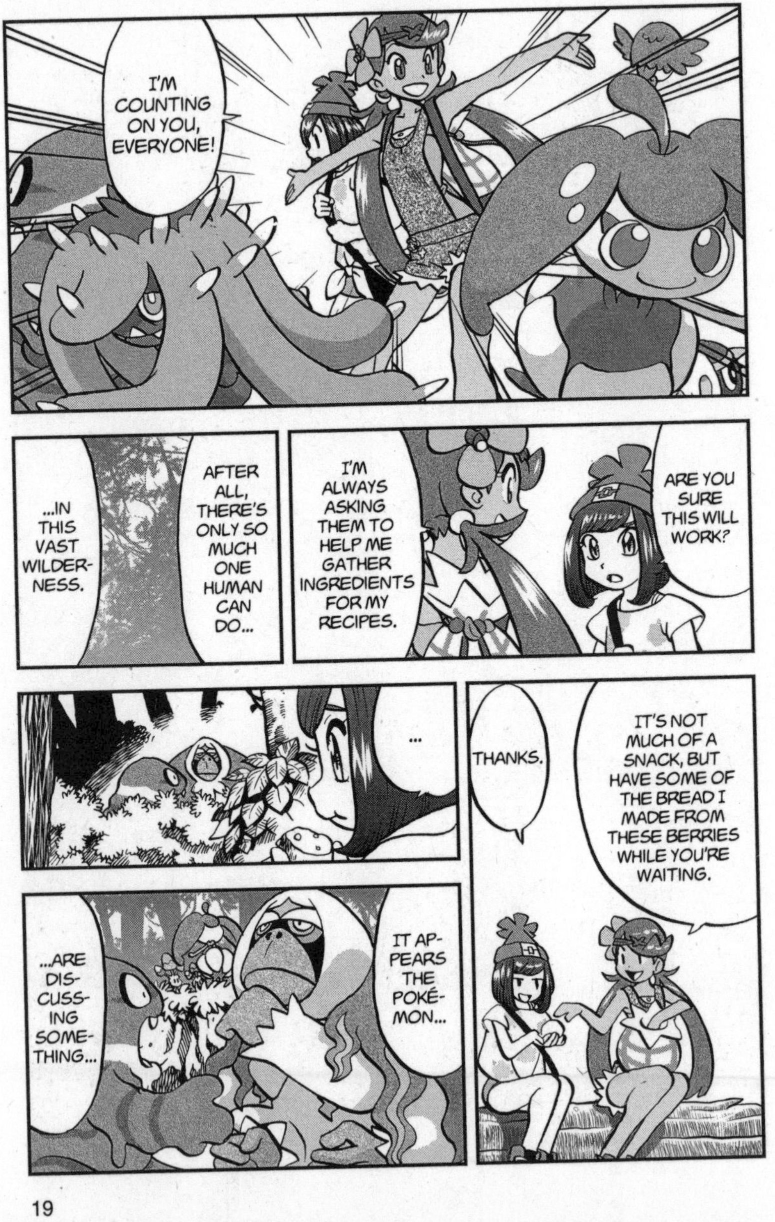
I'M COUNTING ON YOU, EVERYONE!
ARE YOU SURE THIS WILL WORK?
I'M ALWAYS ASKING THEM TO HELP ME GATHER INGREDIENTS FOR MY RECIPES.
AFTER ALL, THERE'S ONLY SO MUCH ONE HUMAN CAN DO...
...IN THIS VAST WILDER-NESS.
IT'S NOT MUCH OF A SNACK, BUT HAVE SOME OF THE BREAD I MADE FROM THESE BERRIES WHILE YOU'RE WAITING.
THANKS.
...
IT AP-PEARS THE POKÉ-MON...
...ARE DIS-CUSS-ING SOME-THING...

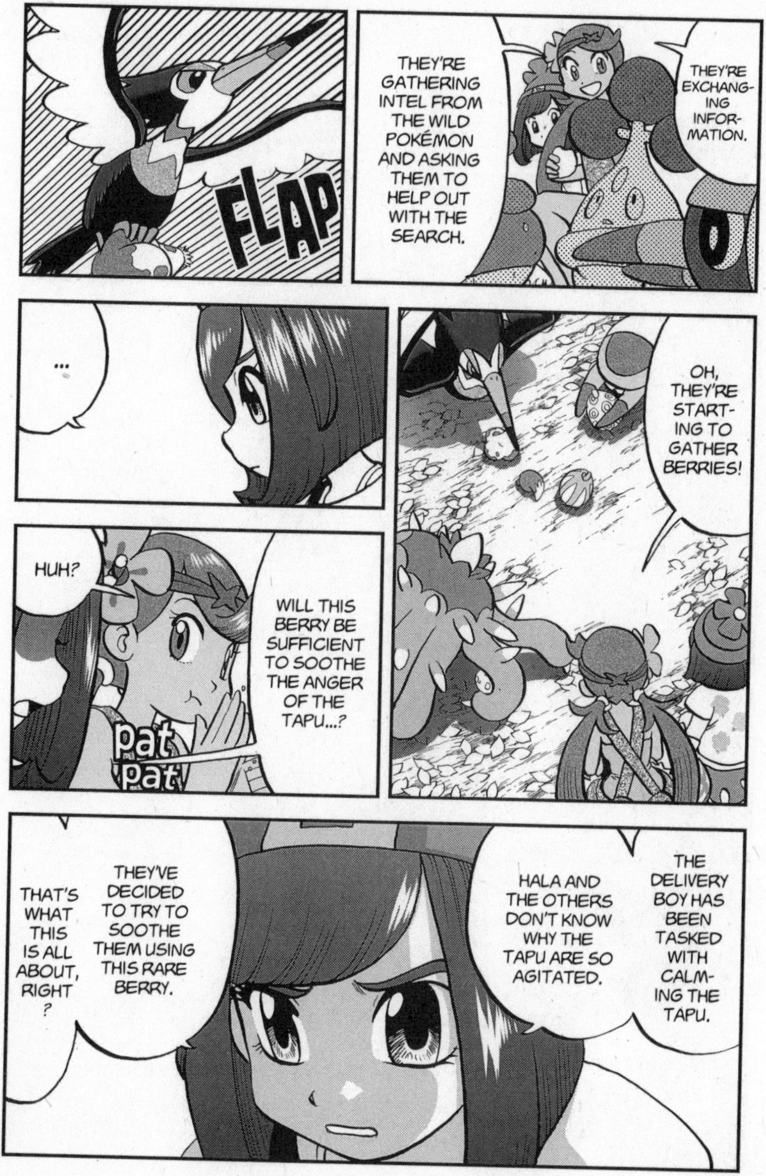
THEY'RE EXCHANGING INFORMATION.
THEY'RE GATHERING INTEL FROM THE WILD POKéMON AND ASKING THEM TO HELP OUT WITH THE SEARCH.
FLAP
OH, THEY'RE STARTING TO GATHER BERRIES!
...
WILL THIS BERRY BE SUFFICIENT TO SOOTHE THE ANGER OF THE TAPU...?
HUH?
pat pat
THE DELIVERY BOY HAS BEEN TASKED WITH CALMING THE TAPU.
HALA AND THE OTHERS DON'T KNOW WHY THE TAPU ARE SO AGITATED.
THEY'VE DECIDED TO TRY TO SOOTHE THEM USING THIS RARE BERRY.
THAT'S WHAT THIS IS ALL ABOUT, RIGHT?

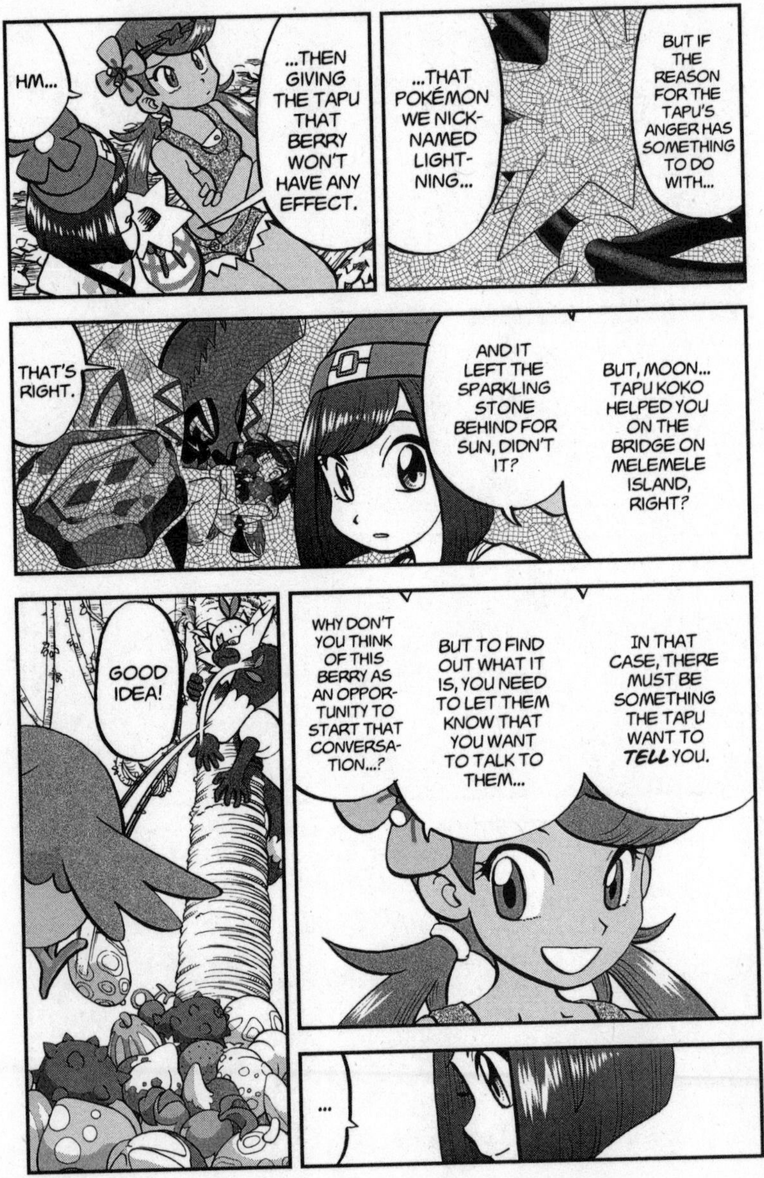
BUT IF THE REASON FOR THE TAPU'S ANGER HAS SOMETHING TO DO WITH...
...THAT POKÉMON WE NICKNAMED LIGHTNING...
...THEN GIVING THE TAPU THAT BERRY WON'T HAVE ANY EFFECT.
HM...
BUT, MOON... TAPU KOKO HELPED YOU ON THE BRIDGE ON MELEMELE ISLAND, RIGHT?
AND IT LEFT THE SPARKLING STONE BEHIND FOR SUN, DIDN'T IT?
THAT'S RIGHT.
IN THAT CASE, THERE MUST BE SOMETHING THE TAPU WANT TO *TELL* YOU.
BUT TO FIND OUT WHAT IT IS, YOU NEED TO LET THEM KNOW THAT YOU WANT TO TALK TO THEM...
WHY DON'T YOU THINK OF THIS BERRY AS AN OPPORTUNITY TO START THAT CONVERSATION...?
...
GOOD IDEA!

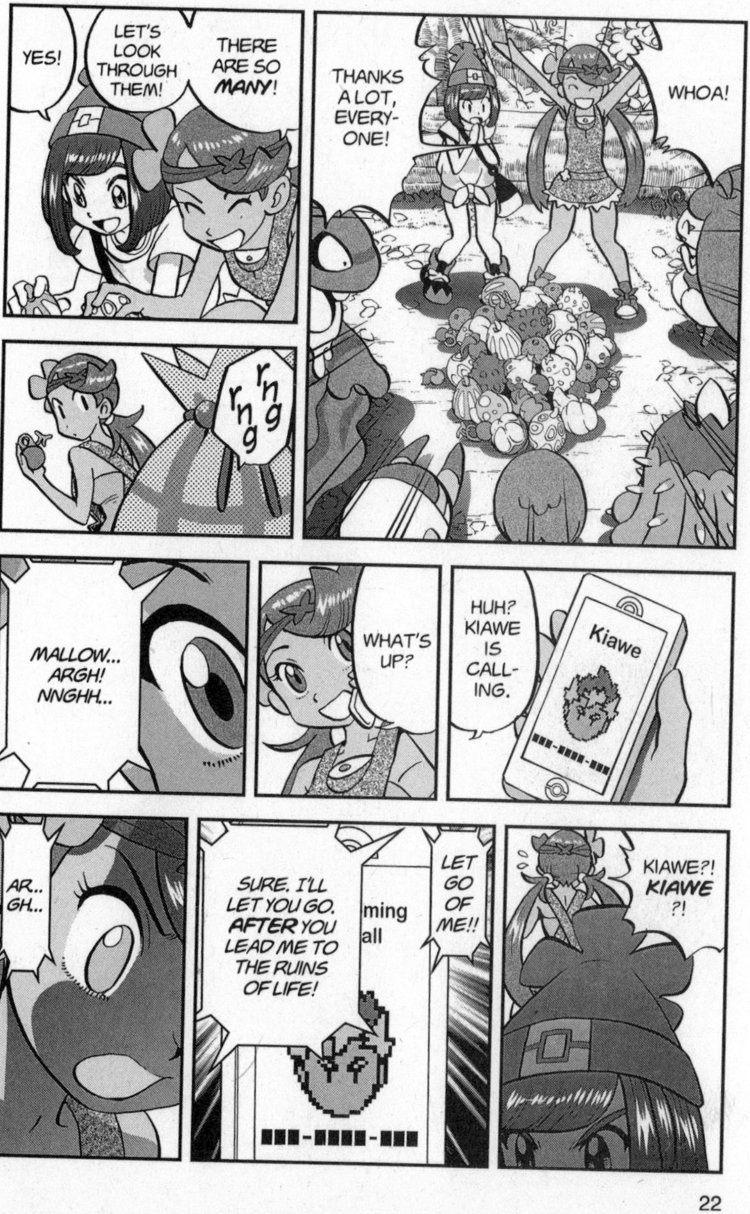
WHOA!
THANKS A LOT, EVERY-ONE!
THERE ARE SO MANY!
LET'S LOOK THROUGH THEM!
YES!
rng rng
HUH? KIAWE IS CALL-ING.
Kiawe
WHAT'S UP?
MALLOW... ARGH! NNGHH...
KIAWE?! KIAWE ?!
LET GO OF ME!!
SURE. I'LL LET YOU GO. AFTER YOU LEAD ME TO THE RUINS OF LIFE!
AR... GH...

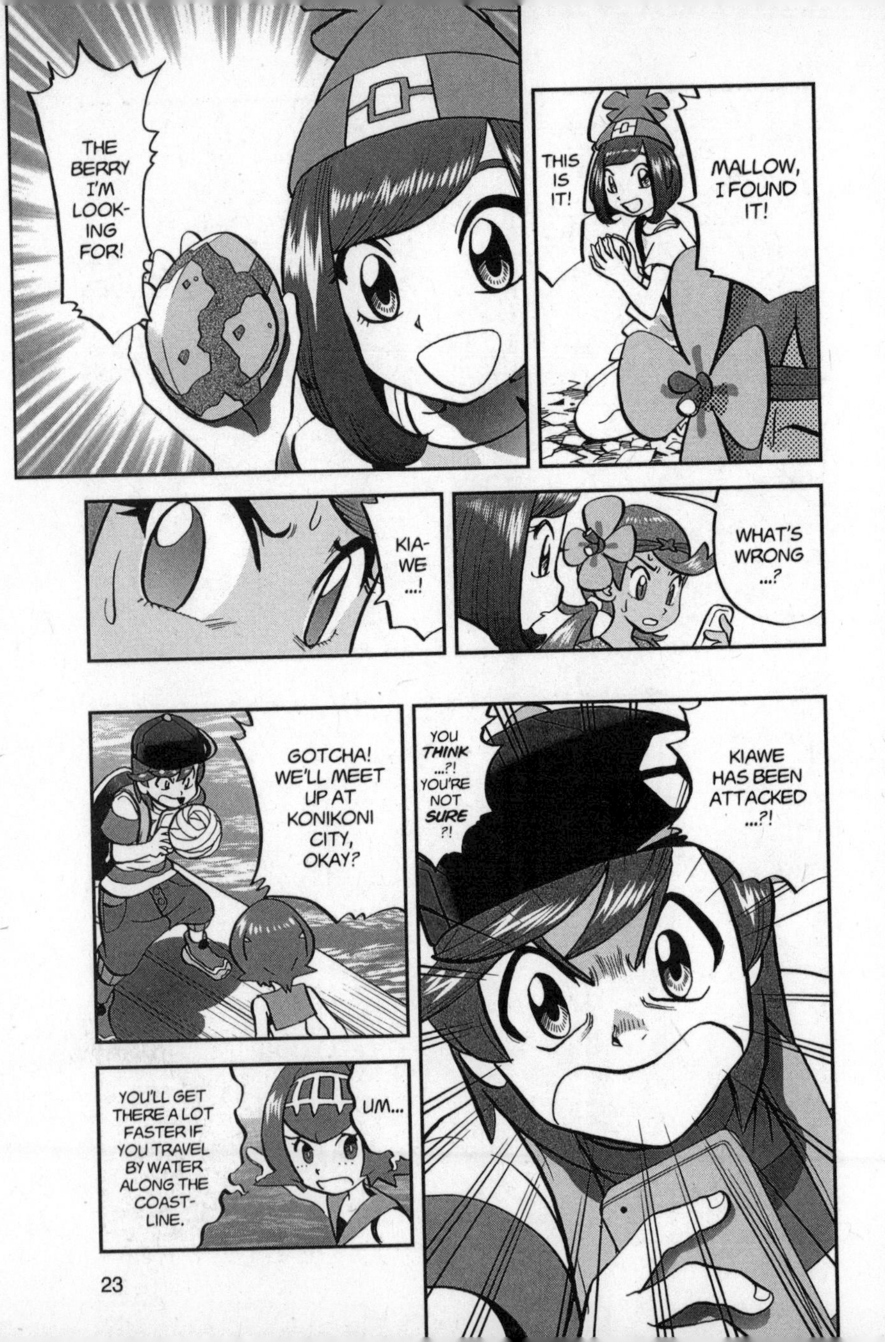

MALLOW, I FOUND IT!
THIS IS IT!
THE BERRY I'M LOOKING FOR!
WHAT'S WRONG ...?
KIAWE ...!
KIAWE HAS BEEN ATTACKED ...?!
YOU ***THINK*** ...?! YOU'RE NOT ***SURE***?!
GOTCHA! WE'LL MEET UP AT KONIKONI CITY, OKAY?
UM...
YOU'LL GET THERE A LOT FASTER IF YOU TRAVEL BY WATER ALONG THE COASTLINE.

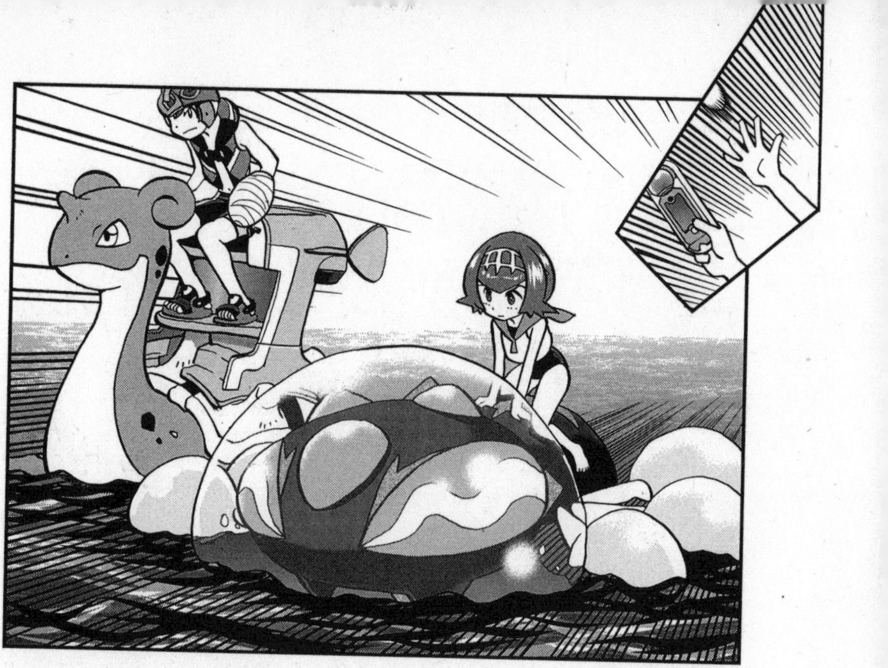

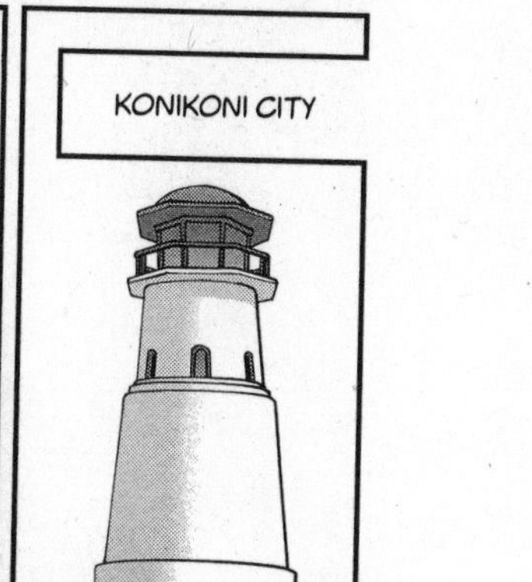
KONIKONI CITY

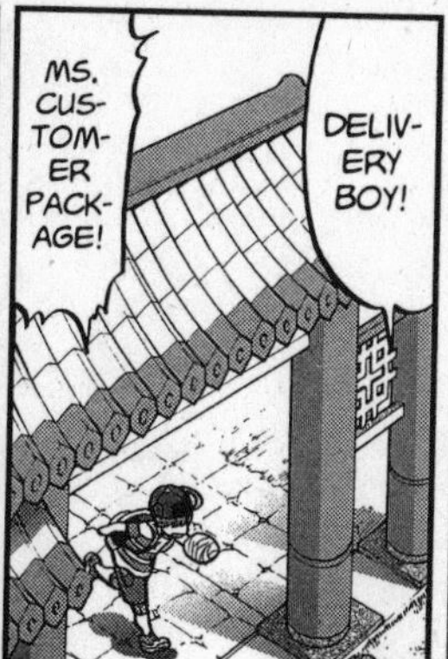
DELIV-
ERY
BOY!
MS.
CUS-
TOM-
ER
PACK-
AGE!

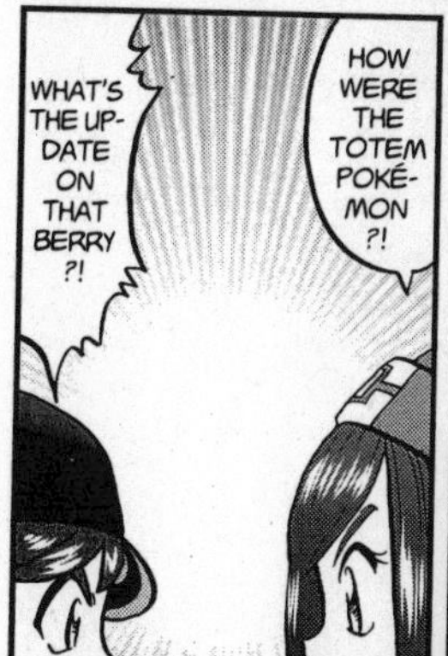
HOW
WERE
THE
TOTEM
POKÉ-
MON
?!
WHAT'S
THE UP-
DATE
ON
THAT
BERRY
?!

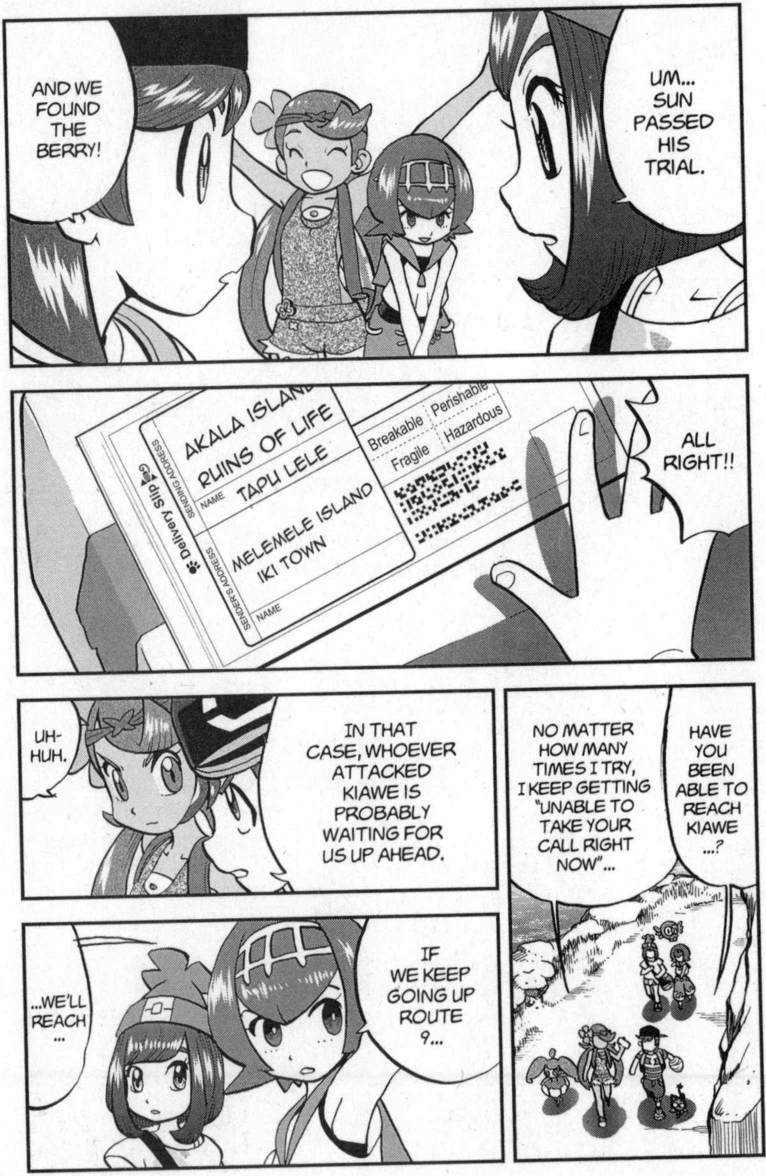
UM... SUN PASSED HIS TRIAL.
AND WE FOUND THE BERRY!
ALL RIGHT!!
Delivery Slip
SENDING ADDRESS
AKALA ISLAND
RUINS OF LIFE
NAME
TAPU LELE
Breakable
Perishable
Fragile
Hazardous
SENDER'S ADDRESS
MELEMELE ISLAND
IKI TOWN
NAME
HAVE YOU BEEN ABLE TO REACH KIAWE ...?
NO MATTER HOW MANY TIMES I TRY, I KEEP GETTING "UNABLE TO TAKE YOUR CALL RIGHT NOW"...
IN THAT CASE, WHOEVER ATTACKED KIAWE IS PROBABLY WAITING FOR US UP AHEAD.
UH-HUH.
IF WE KEEP GOING UP ROUTE 9...
...WE'LL REACH ...

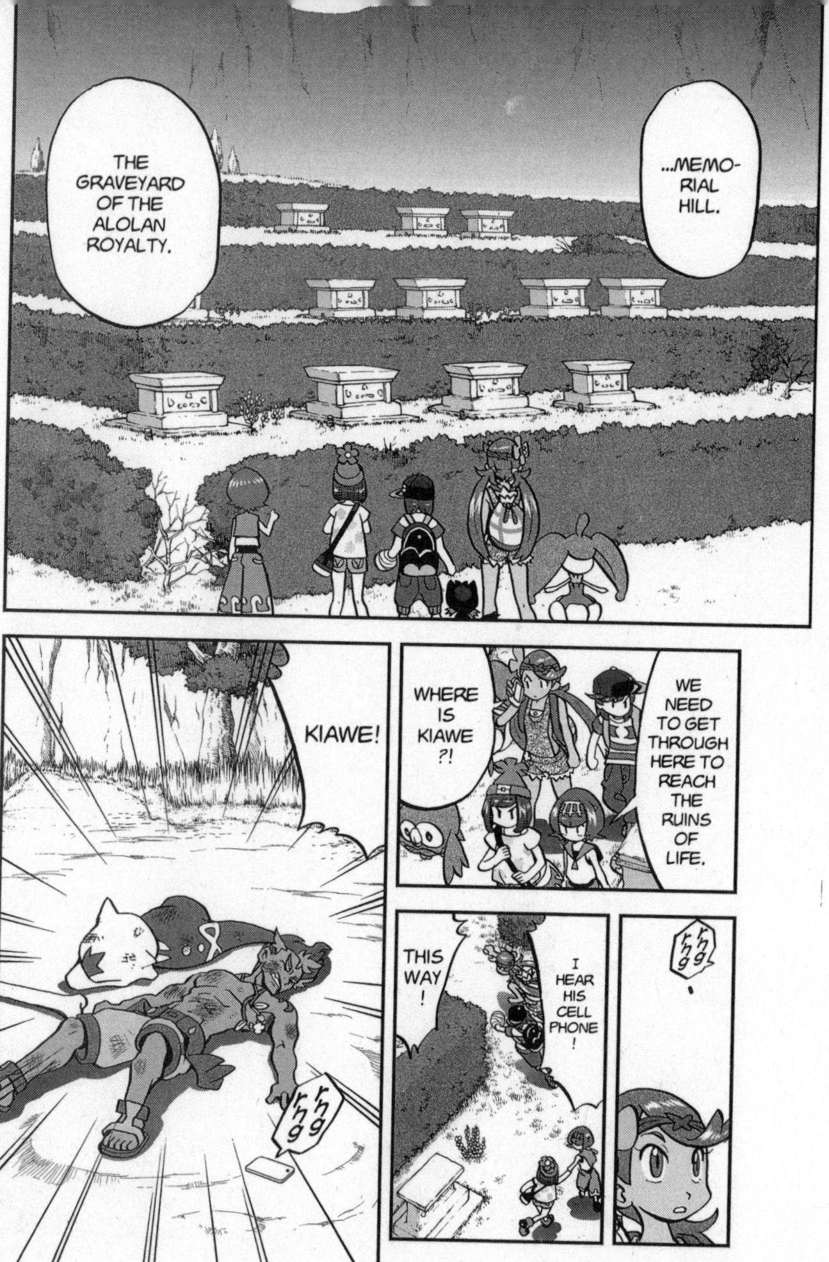
...MEMO-RIAL HILL.
THE GRAVEYARD OF THE ALOLAN ROYALTY.
WE NEED TO GET THROUGH HERE TO REACH THE RUINS OF LIFE.
WHERE IS KIAWE ?!
rng rng
I HEAR HIS CELL PHONE !
THIS WAY !
KIAWE!
rng rng

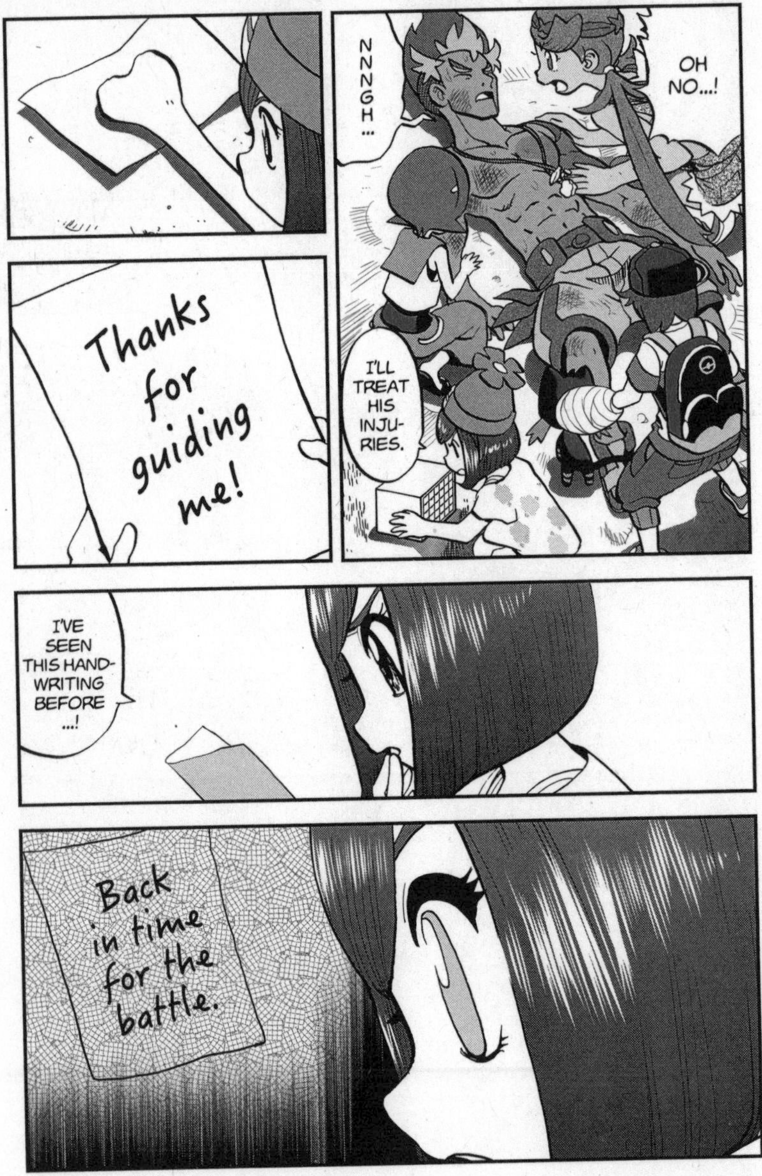
OH NO...!
NNNGH...
I'LL TREAT HIS INJURIES.
Thanks for guiding me!
I'VE SEEN THIS HANDWRITING BEFORE...!
Back in time for the battle.

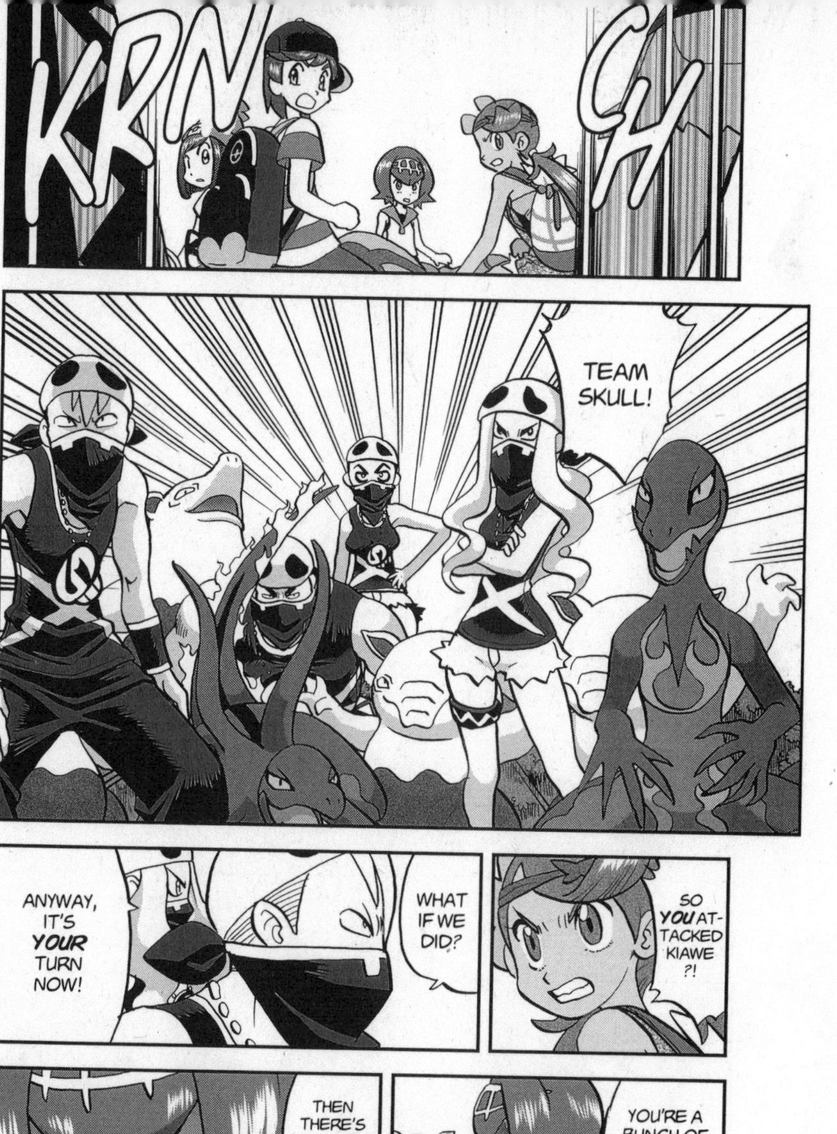
KRNCH
TEAM SKULL!
SO YOU ATTACKED KIAWE?!
WHAT IF WE DID?
ANYWAY, IT'S YOUR TURN NOW!
YOU'RE A BUNCH OF ALOLAN THUGS, AREN'T YOU?
THEN THERE'S NO NEED FOR ME TO GO EASY ON YOU!

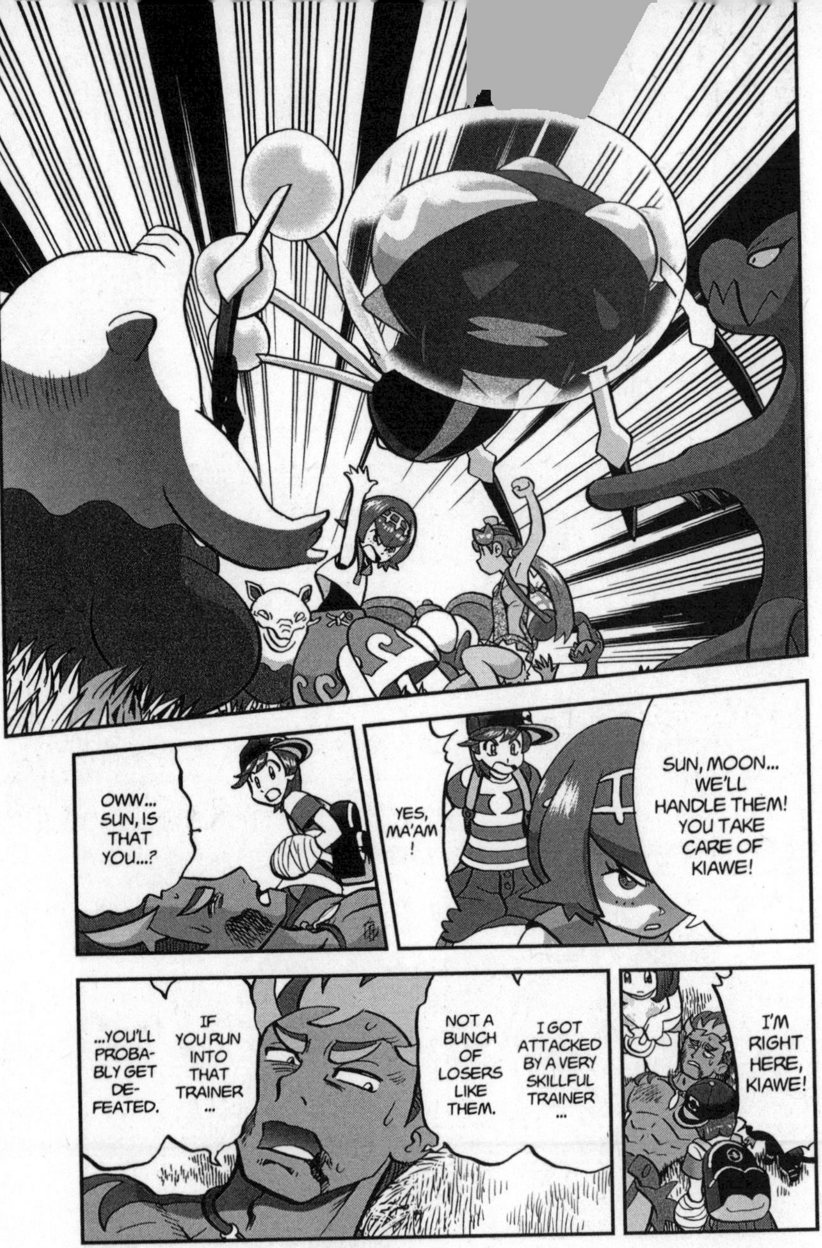
SUN, MOON... WE'LL HANDLE THEM! YOU TAKE CARE OF KIAWE!
YES, MA'AM!
OWW... SUN, IS THAT YOU...?
I'M RIGHT HERE, KIAWE!
I GOT ATTACKED BY A VERY SKILLFUL TRAINER...
NOT A BUNCH OF LOSERS LIKE THEM.
IF YOU RUN INTO THAT TRAINER...
...YOU'LL PROBA-BLY GET DE-FEATED.

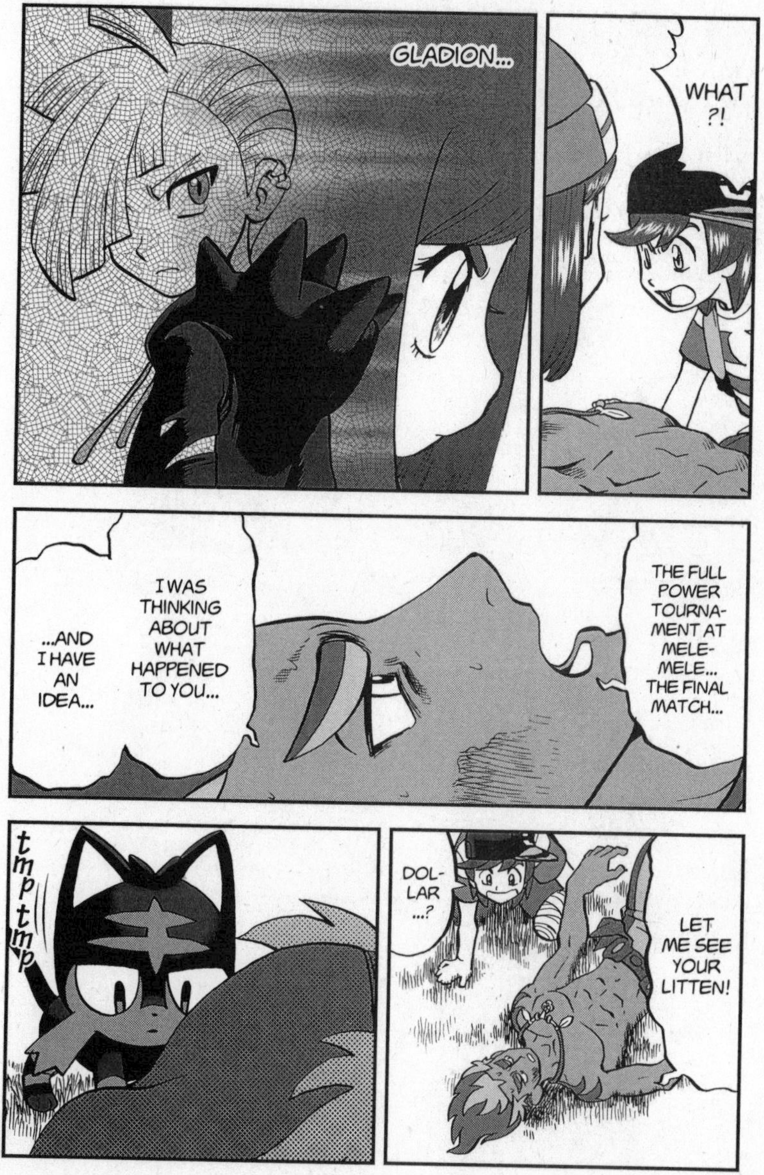

WHAT ?!
GLADION...
THE FULL POWER TOURNAMENT AT MELE-MELE... THE FINAL MATCH...
I WAS THINKING ABOUT WHAT HAPPENED TO YOU...
...AND I HAVE AN IDEA...
LET ME SEE YOUR LITTEN!
DOL-LAR ...?
tmp tmp

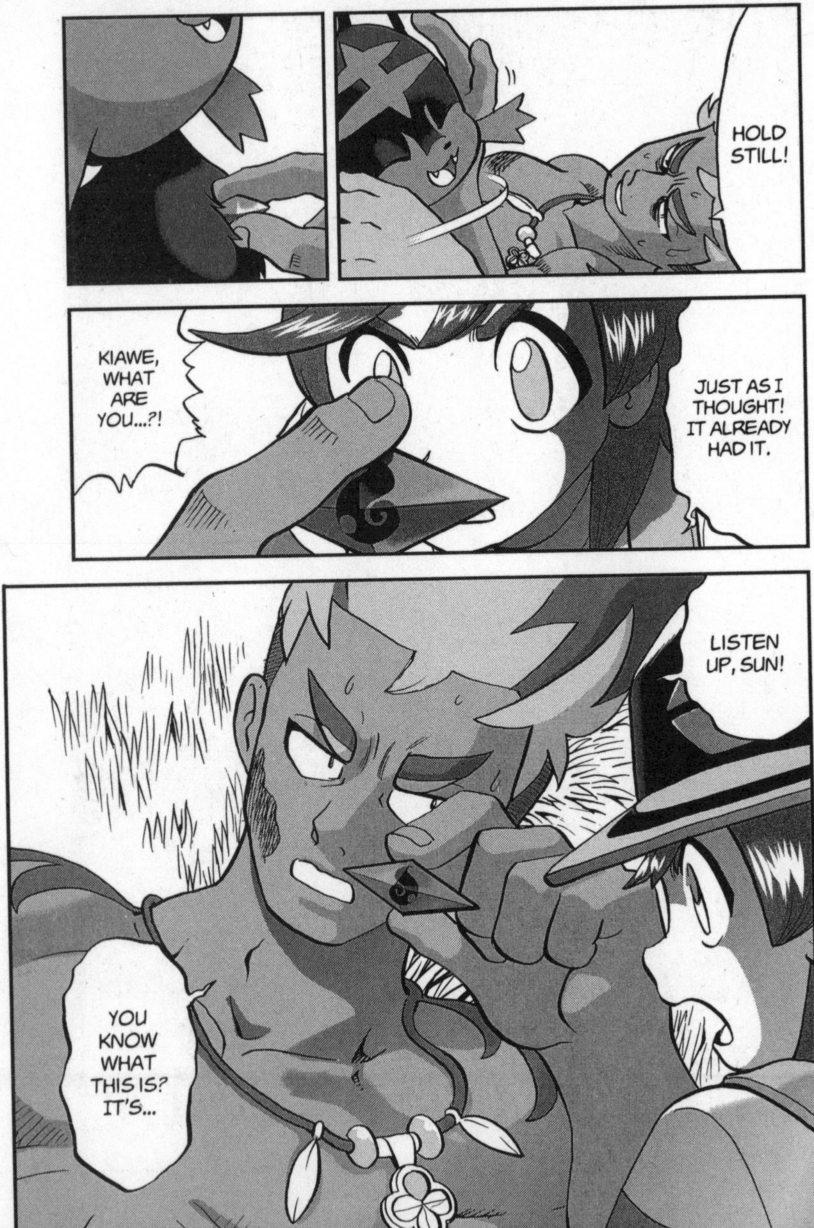
HOLD STILL!
JUST AS I THOUGHT! IT ALREADY HAD IT.
KIAWE, WHAT ARE YOU...?!
LISTEN UP, SUN!
YOU KNOW WHAT THIS IS? IT'S...

Trial Captain

Trial Captains are skilled Trainers on the island. They were originally in charge of testing the skills of the Trainers in the Island Challenge, but since the Island Challenge hasn't been held in the past few years, they are really bored...

Guide to Alola 10

Adventure 12
The Wild Full-Power Pose of Fire

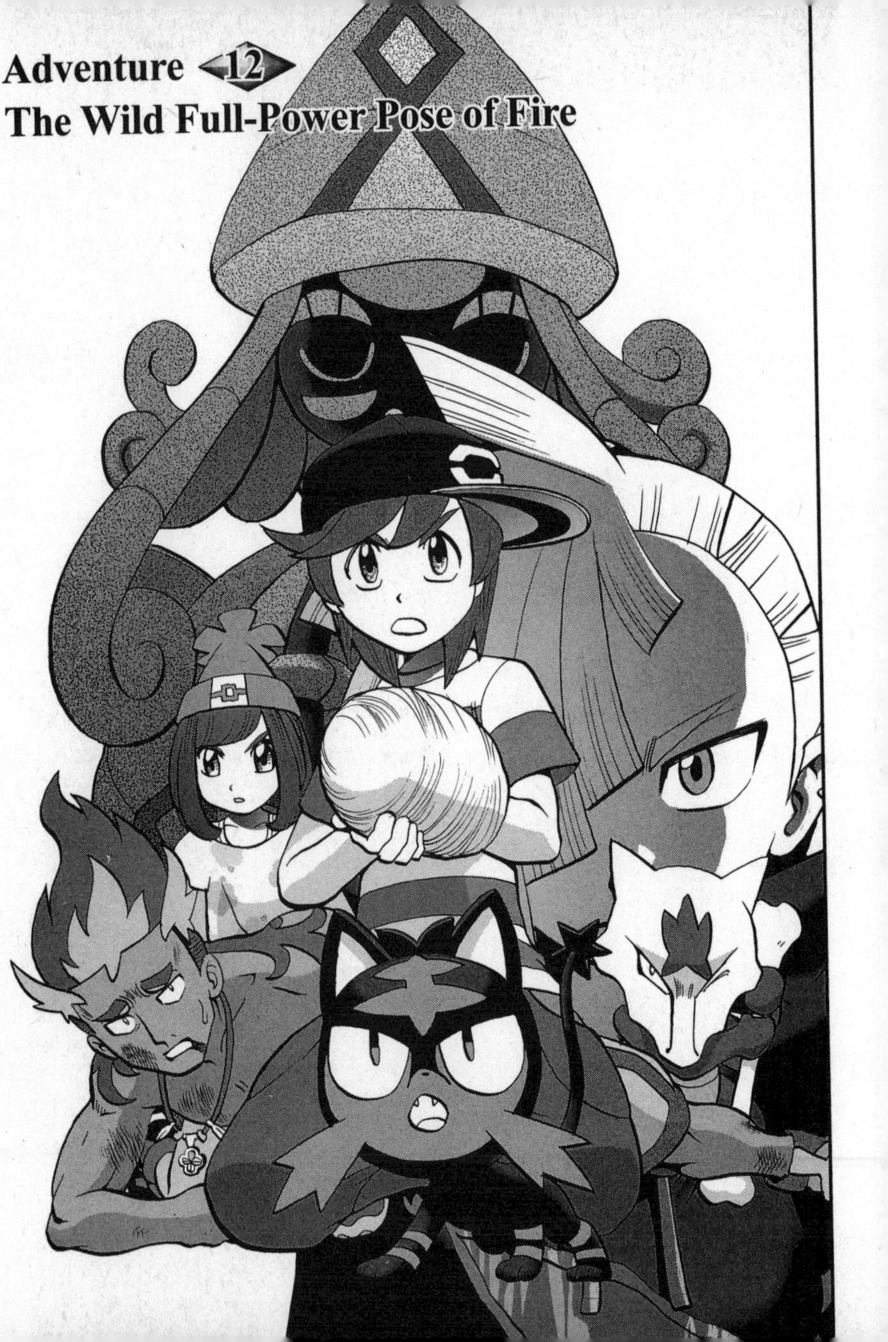

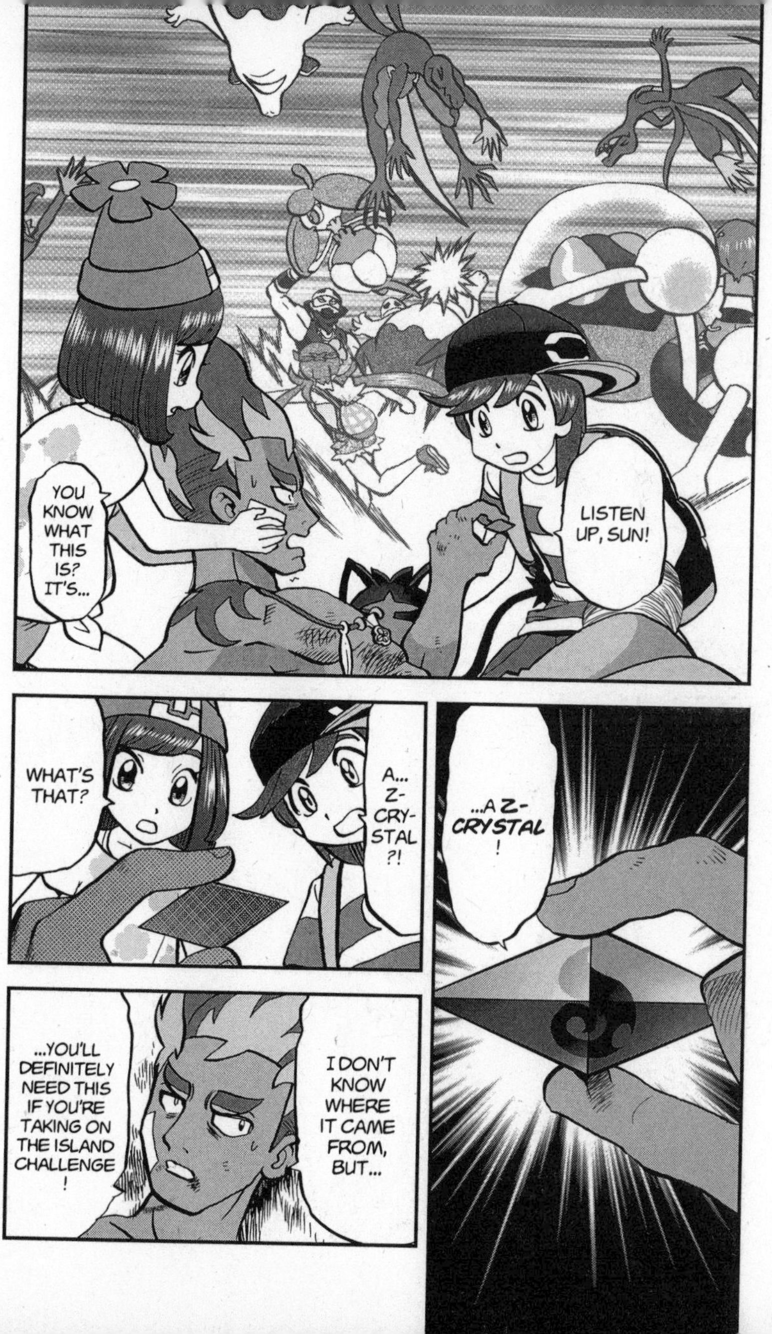
LISTEN UP, SUN!
YOU KNOW WHAT THIS IS? IT'S...
...A Z-CRYSTAL!
A... Z-CRYSTAL?!
WHAT'S THAT?
I DON'T KNOW WHERE IT CAME FROM, BUT...
...YOU'LL DEFINITELY NEED THIS IF YOU'RE TAKING ON THE ISLAND CHALLENGE!

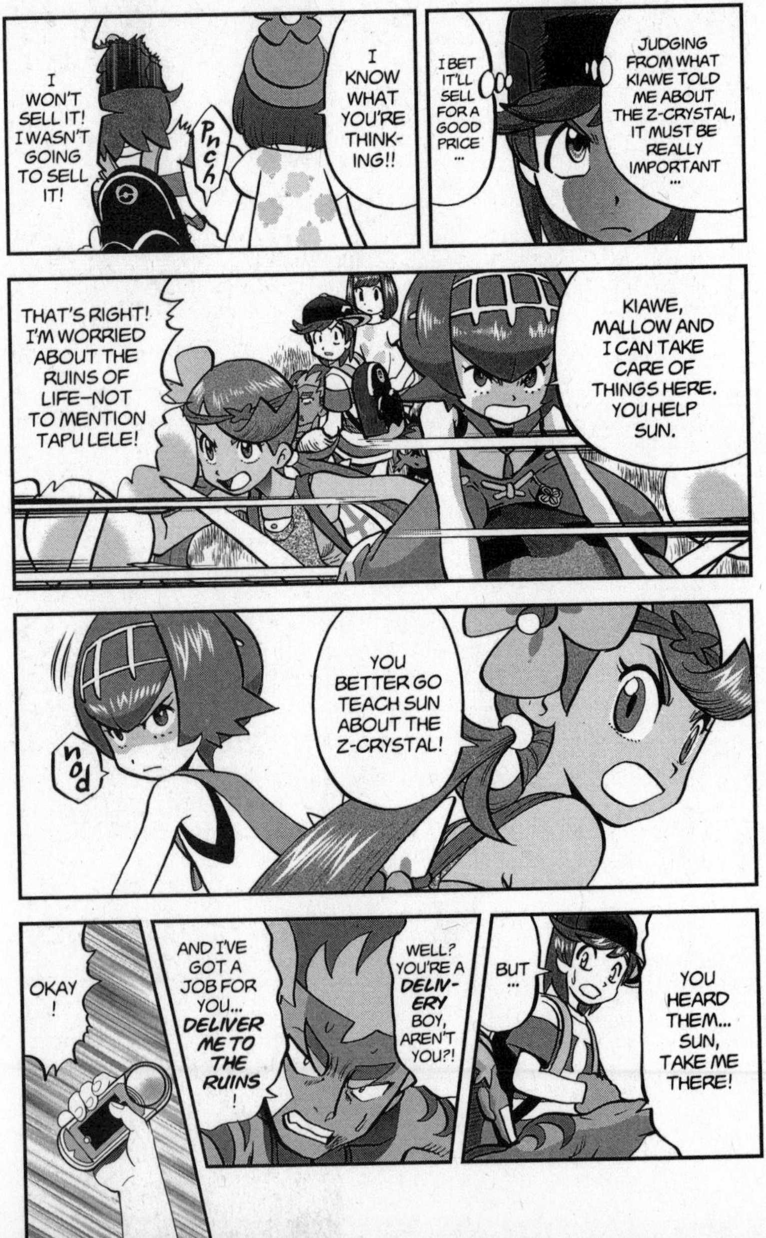
JUDGING FROM WHAT KIAWE TOLD ME ABOUT THE Z-CRYSTAL, IT MUST BE REALLY IMPORTANT...
I BET IT'LL SELL FOR A GOOD PRICE...
I KNOW WHAT YOU'RE THINKING!!
Pnch
I WON'T SELL IT! I WASN'T GOING TO SELL IT!
KIAWE, MALLOW AND I CAN TAKE CARE OF THINGS HERE. YOU HELP SUN.
THAT'S RIGHT! I'M WORRIED ABOUT THE RUINS OF LIFE—NOT TO MENTION TAPU LELE!
YOU BETTER GO TEACH SUN ABOUT THE Z-CRYSTAL!
nod
YOU HEARD THEM... SUN, TAKE ME THERE!
BUT...
WELL? YOU'RE A ***DELIVERY*** BOY, AREN'T YOU?!
AND I'VE GOT A JOB FOR YOU... ***DELIVER ME TO THE RUINS***!
OKAY!

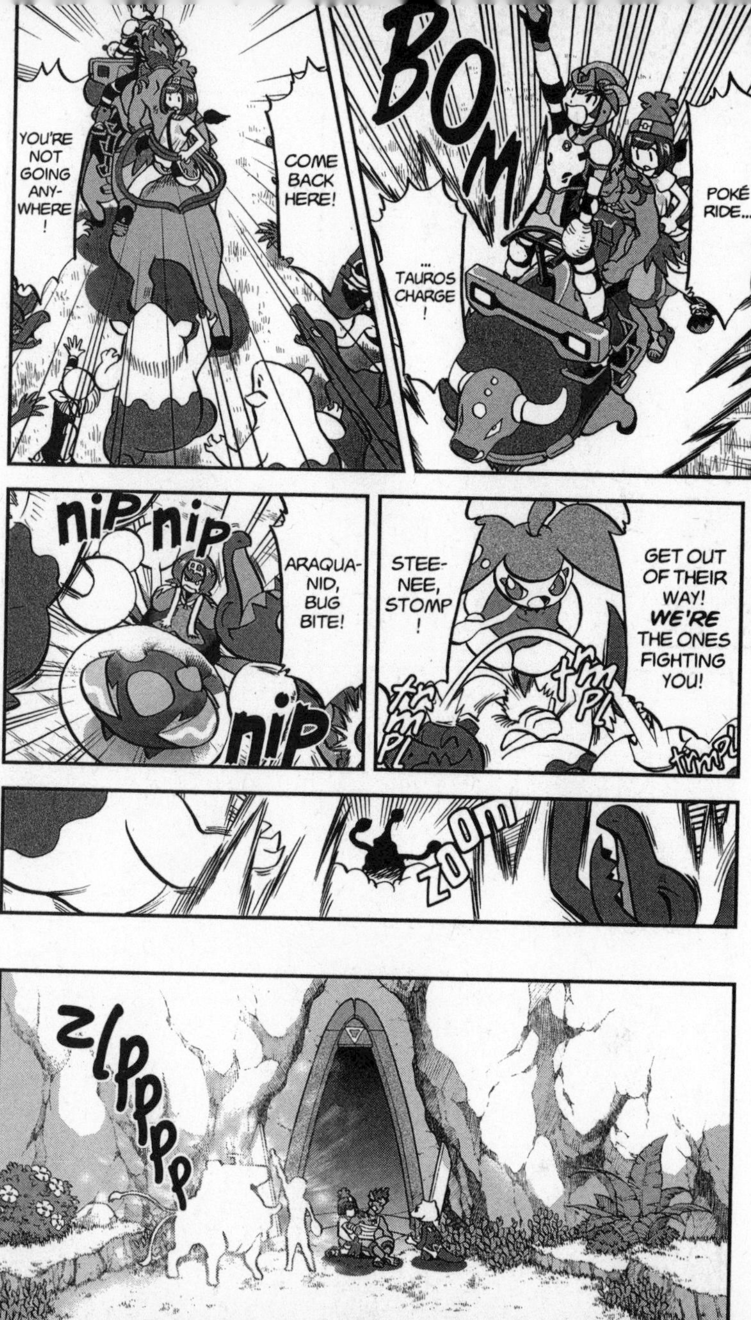
POKÉ RIDE...
BOM
...TAUROS CHARGE!
COME BACK HERE!
YOU'RE NOT GOING ANYWHERE!
GET OUT OF THEIR WAY! ***WE'RE*** THE ONES FIGHTING YOU!
STEE-NEE, STOMP!
tmpl tmpl tmpl tmpl
ARAQUANID, BUG BITE!
nip nip
nip
zoom
zipppp

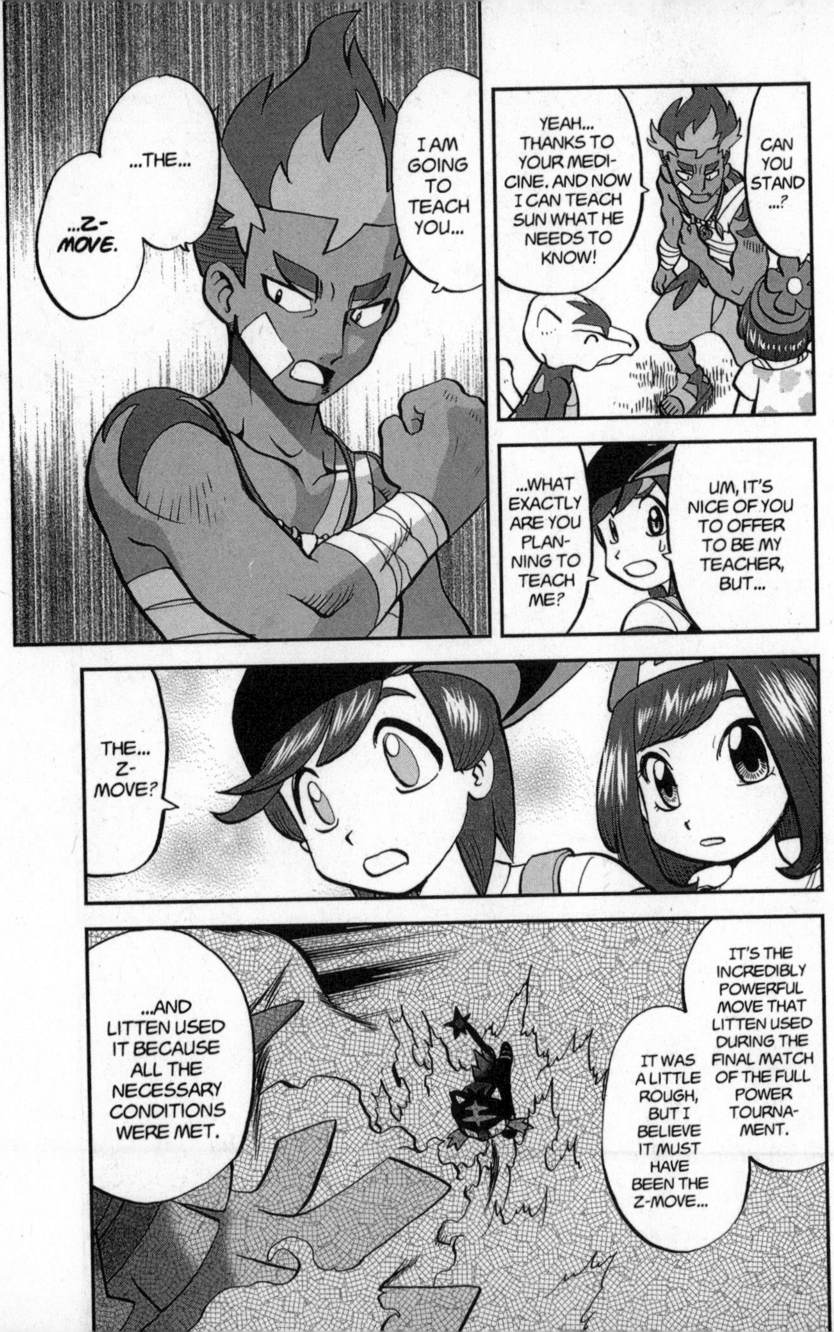
CAN YOU STAND ...?
YEAH... THANKS TO YOUR MEDICINE. AND NOW I CAN TEACH SUN WHAT HE NEEDS TO KNOW!
UM, IT'S NICE OF YOU TO OFFER TO BE MY TEACHER, BUT...
...WHAT EXACTLY ARE YOU PLANNING TO TEACH ME?
I AM GOING TO TEACH YOU...
...THE...
...Z-MOVE.
THE... Z-MOVE?
IT'S THE INCREDIBLY POWERFUL MOVE THAT LITTEN USED DURING THE FINAL MATCH OF THE FULL POWER TOURNAMENT.
IT WAS A LITTLE ROUGH, BUT I BELIEVE IT MUST HAVE BEEN THE Z-MOVE...
...AND LITTEN USED IT BECAUSE ALL THE NECESSARY CONDITIONS WERE MET.

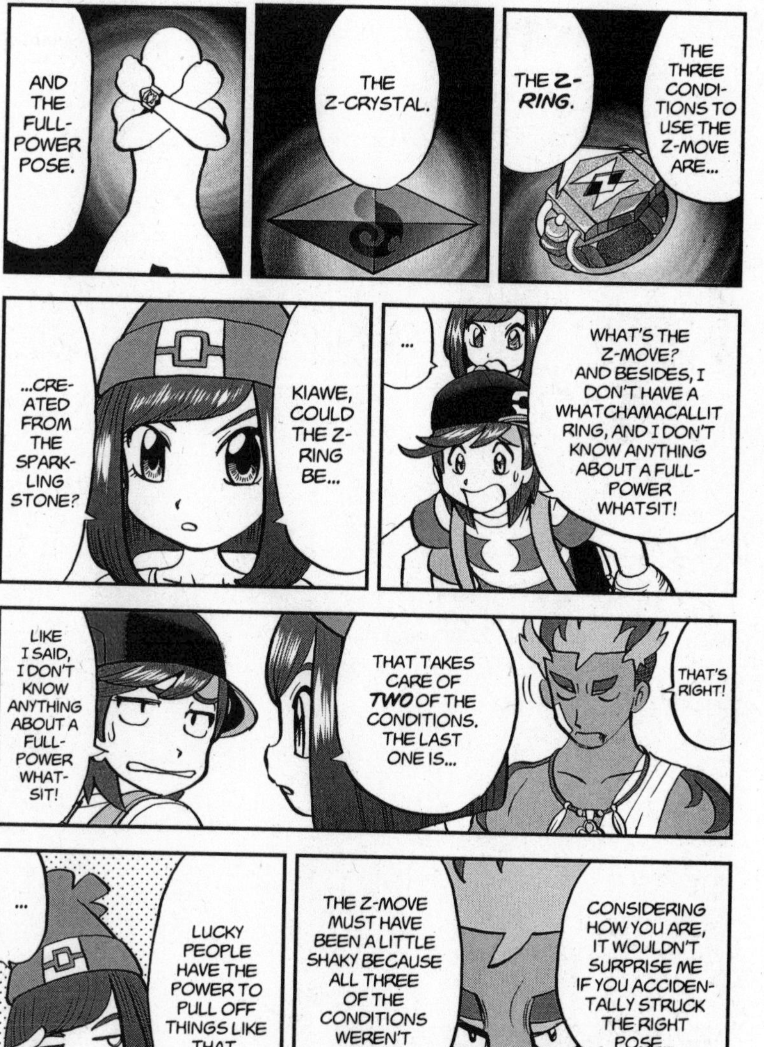
THE THREE CONDITIONS TO USE THE Z-MOVE ARE...
THE **Z-RING**.
THE Z-CRYSTAL.
AND THE FULL-POWER POSE.
WHAT'S THE Z-MOVE? AND BESIDES, I DON'T HAVE A WHATCHAMACALLIT RING, AND I DON'T KNOW ANYTHING ABOUT A FULL-POWER WHATSIT!
...
KIAWE, COULD THE Z-RING BE...
...CREATED FROM THE SPARKLING STONE?
THAT'S RIGHT!
THAT TAKES CARE OF ***TWO*** OF THE CONDITIONS. THE LAST ONE IS...
LIKE I SAID, I DON'T KNOW ANYTHING ABOUT A FULL-POWER WHATSIT!
CONSIDERING HOW YOU ARE, IT WOULDN'T SURPRISE ME IF YOU ACCIDENTALLY STRUCK THE RIGHT POSE...
THE Z-MOVE MUST HAVE BEEN A LITTLE SHAKY BECAUSE ALL THREE OF THE CONDITIONS WEREN'T ***EXACTLY*** RIGHT.
LUCKY PEOPLE HAVE THE POWER TO PULL OFF THINGS LIKE THAT.
...

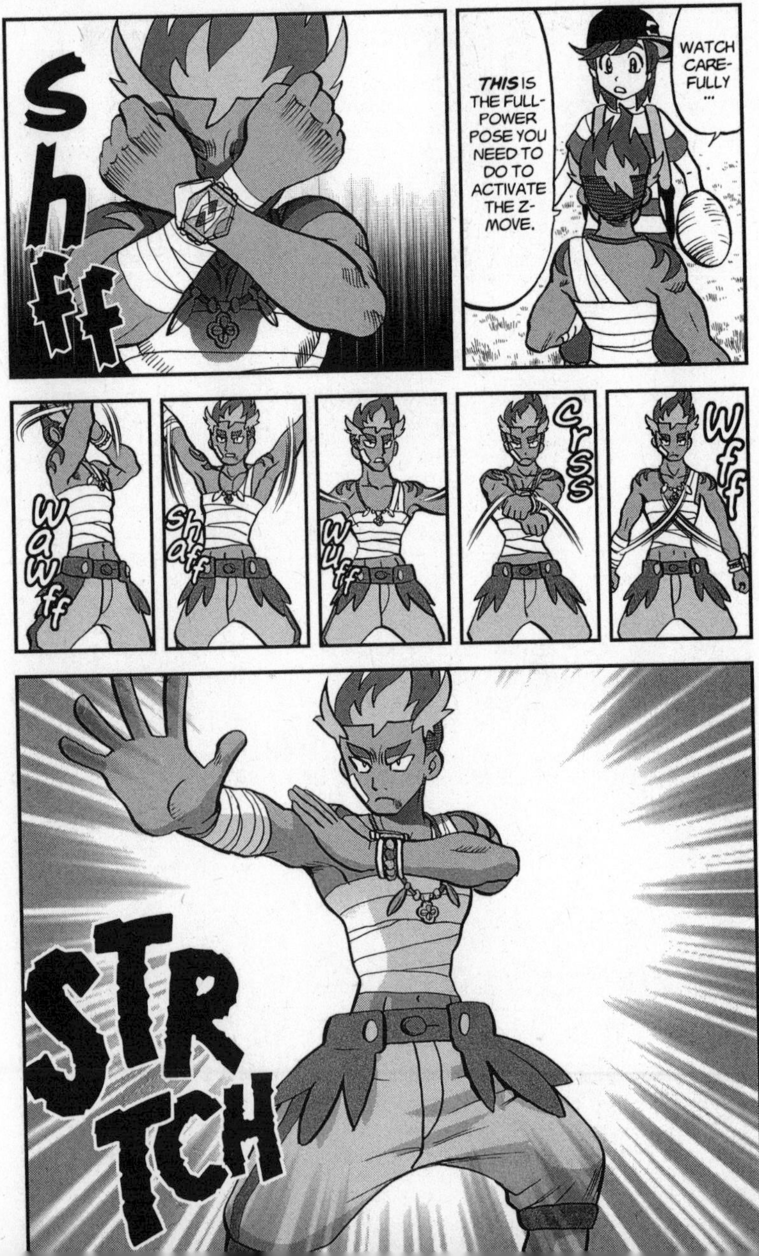
WATCH CARE-FULLY ...
THIS IS THE FULL-POWER POSE YOU NEED TO DO TO ACTIVATE THE Z-MOVE.
shff
wff
crss
wuff
shaff
wawff
STRTCH

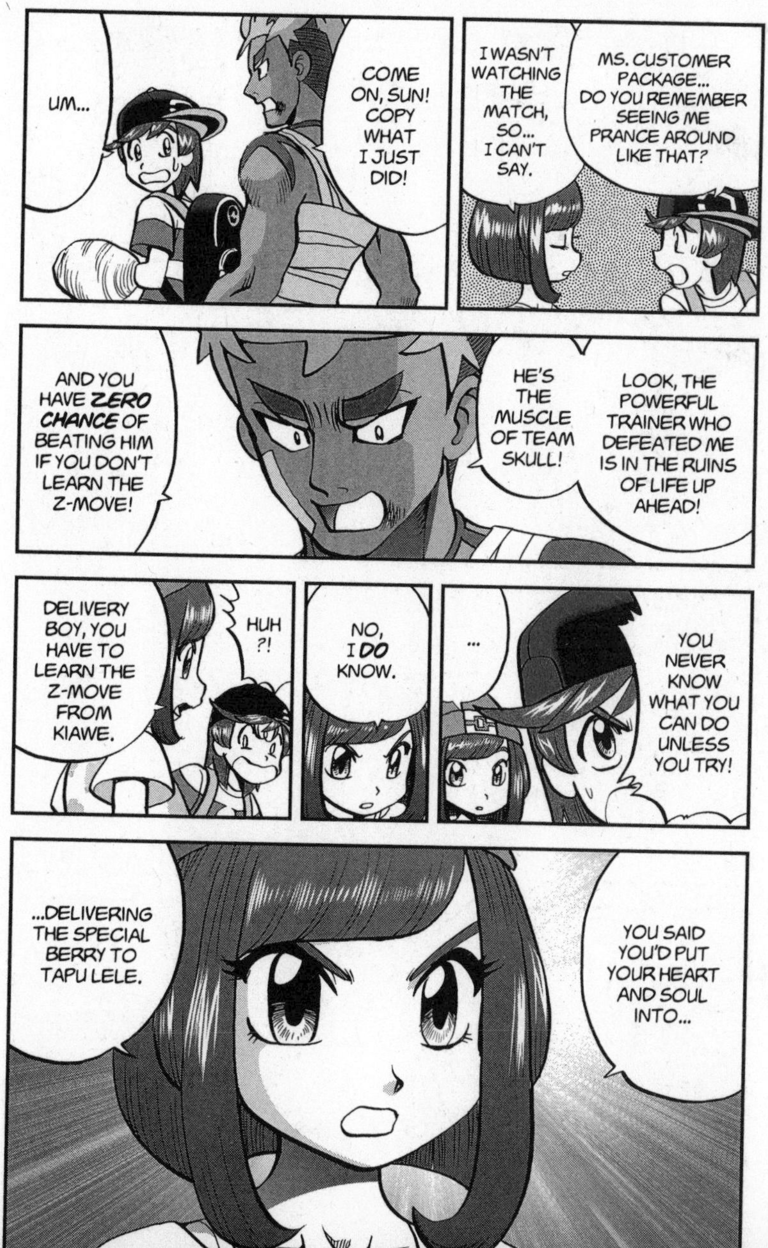
MS. CUSTOMER PACKAGE... DO YOU REMEMBER SEEING ME PRANCE AROUND LIKE THAT?
I WASN'T WATCHING THE MATCH, SO... I CAN'T SAY.
COME ON, SUN! COPY WHAT I JUST DID!
UM...
LOOK, THE POWERFUL TRAINER WHO DEFEATED ME IS IN THE RUINS OF LIFE UP AHEAD!
HE'S THE MUSCLE OF TEAM SKULL!
AND YOU HAVE ZERO CHANCE OF BEATING HIM IF YOU DON'T LEARN THE Z-MOVE!
YOU NEVER KNOW WHAT YOU CAN DO UNLESS YOU TRY!
...
NO, I DO KNOW.
HUH ?!
DELIVERY BOY, YOU HAVE TO LEARN THE Z-MOVE FROM KIAWE.
YOU SAID YOU'D PUT YOUR HEART AND SOUL INTO...
...DELIVERING THE SPECIAL BERRY TO TAPU LELE.

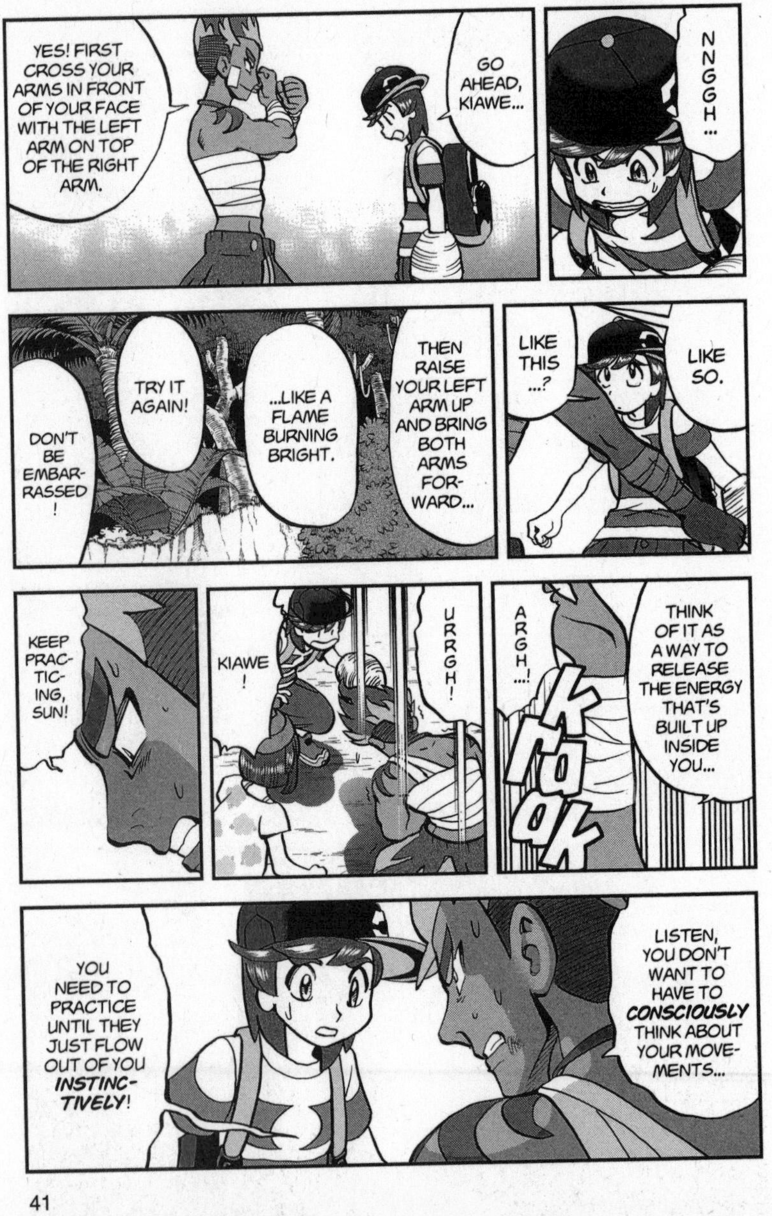
NNGGH...
GO AHEAD, KIAWE...
YES! FIRST CROSS YOUR ARMS IN FRONT OF YOUR FACE WITH THE LEFT ARM ON TOP OF THE RIGHT ARM.
LIKE SO.
LIKE THIS ...?
THEN RAISE YOUR LEFT ARM UP AND BRING BOTH ARMS FORWARD...
...LIKE A FLAME BURNING BRIGHT.
TRY IT AGAIN!
DON'T BE EMBARRASSED!
THINK OF IT AS A WAY TO RELEASE THE ENERGY THAT'S BUILT UP INSIDE YOU...
KRAAK
ARGH...!
URRGH!
KIAWE!
KEEP PRACTICING, SUN!
LISTEN, YOU DON'T WANT TO HAVE TO **CONSCIOUSLY** THINK ABOUT YOUR MOVEMENTS...
YOU NEED TO PRACTICE UNTIL THEY JUST FLOW OUT OF YOU **INSTINCTIVELY**!

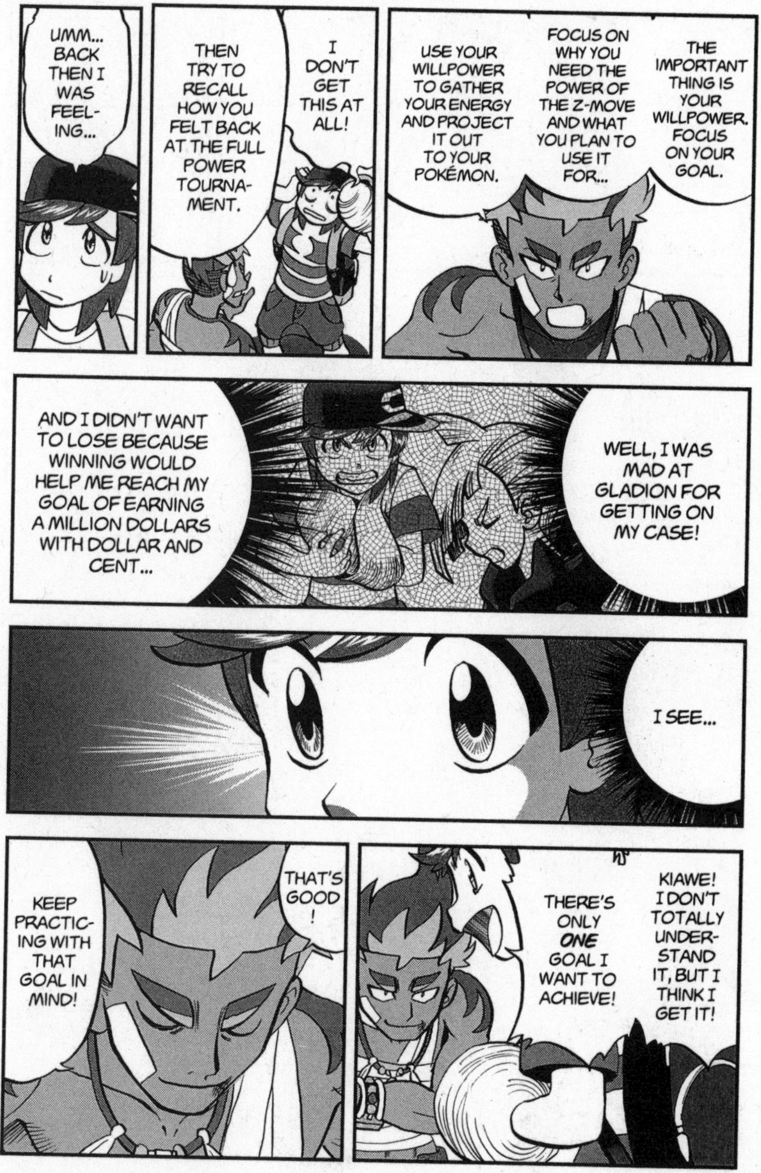
THE IMPORTANT THING IS YOUR WILLPOWER. FOCUS ON YOUR GOAL.
FOCUS ON WHY YOU NEED THE POWER OF THE Z-MOVE AND WHAT YOU PLAN TO USE IT FOR...
USE YOUR WILLPOWER TO GATHER YOUR ENERGY AND PROJECT IT OUT TO YOUR POKÉMON.
I DON'T GET THIS AT ALL!
THEN TRY TO RECALL HOW YOU FELT BACK AT THE FULL POWER TOURNAMENT.
UMM... BACK THEN I WAS FEELING...
WELL, I WAS MAD AT GLADION FOR GETTING ON MY CASE!
AND I DIDN'T WANT TO LOSE BECAUSE WINNING WOULD HELP ME REACH MY GOAL OF EARNING A MILLION DOLLARS WITH DOLLAR AND CENT...
I SEE...
KIAWE! I DON'T TOTALLY UNDERSTAND IT, BUT I THINK I GET IT!
THERE'S ONLY ***ONE*** GOAL I WANT TO ACHIEVE!
THAT'S GOOD!
KEEP PRACTICING WITH THAT GOAL IN MIND!

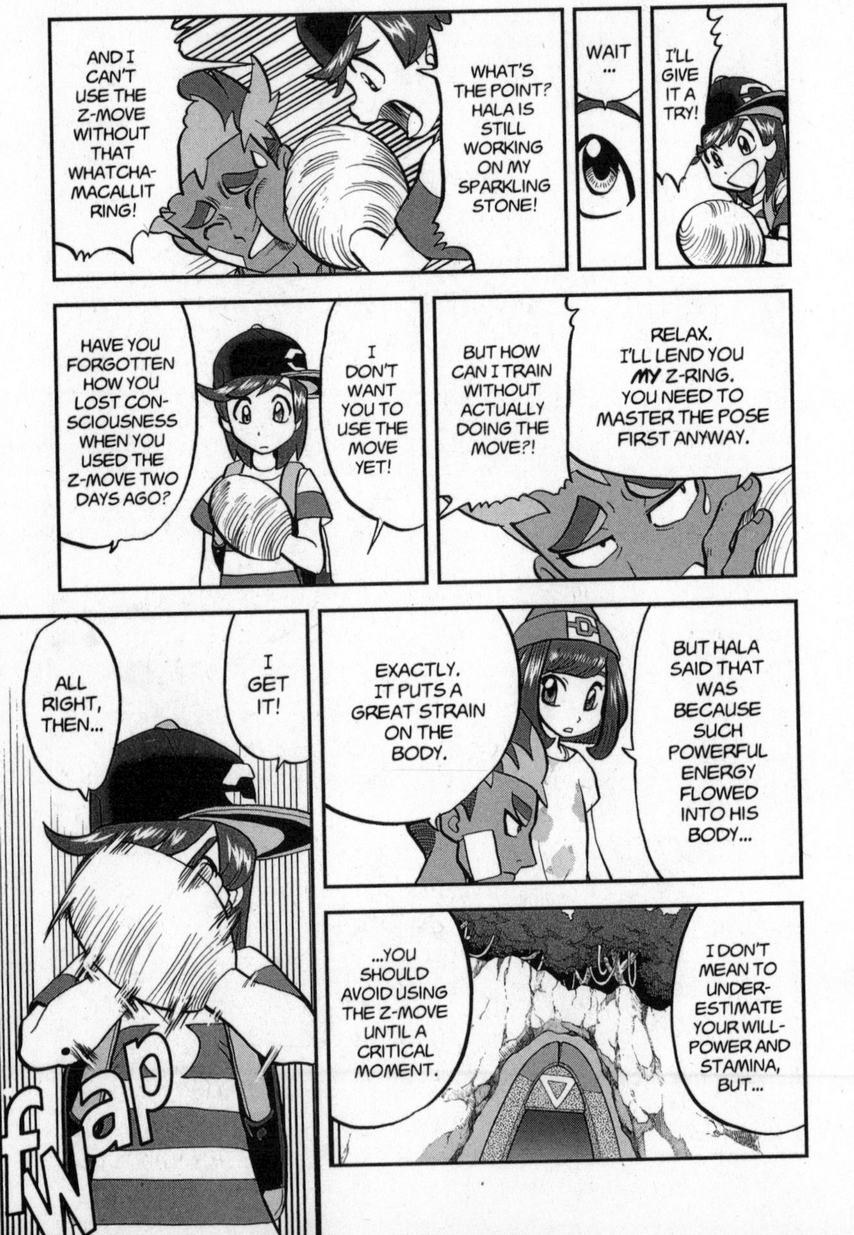
I'LL GIVE IT A TRY!
WAIT ...
WHAT'S THE POINT? HALA IS STILL WORKING ON MY SPARKLING STONE!
AND I CAN'T USE THE Z-MOVE WITHOUT THAT WHATCHA-MACALLIT RING!
RELAX. I'LL LEND YOU MY Z-RING. YOU NEED TO MASTER THE POSE FIRST ANYWAY.
BUT HOW CAN I TRAIN WITHOUT ACTUALLY DOING THE MOVE?!
I DON'T WANT YOU TO USE THE MOVE YET!
HAVE YOU FORGOTTEN HOW YOU LOST CON-SCIOUSNESS WHEN YOU USED THE Z-MOVE TWO DAYS AGO?
BUT HALA SAID THAT WAS BECAUSE SUCH POWERFUL ENERGY FLOWED INTO HIS BODY...
EXACTLY. IT PUTS A GREAT STRAIN ON THE BODY.
I DON'T MEAN TO UNDER-ESTIMATE YOUR WILL-POWER AND STAMINA, BUT...
...YOU SHOULD AVOID USING THE Z-MOVE UNTIL A CRITICAL MOMENT.
I GET IT!
ALL RIGHT, THEN...
fwap

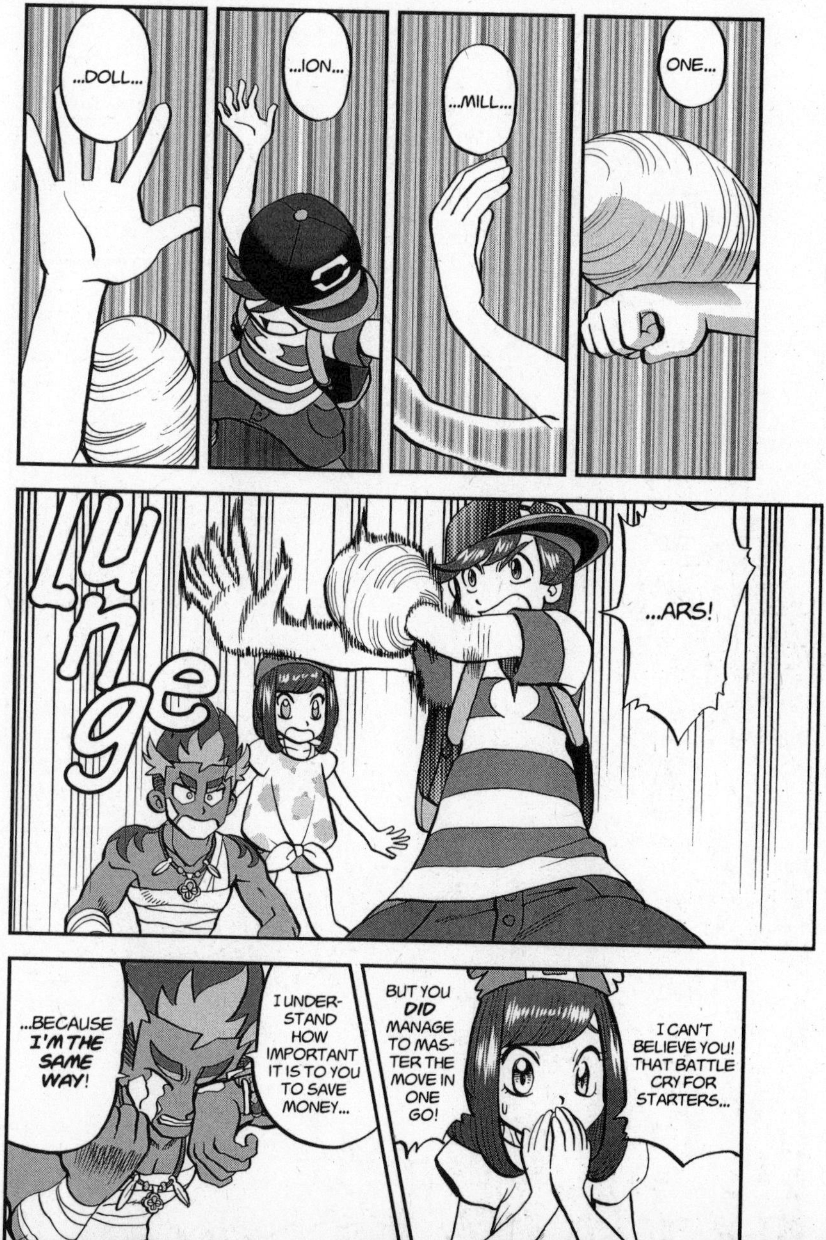
ONE...
...MILL...
...ION...
...DOLL...
...ARS!
lunge
I CAN'T BELIEVE YOU! THAT BATTLE CRY FOR STARTERS...
BUT YOU DID MANAGE TO MASTER THE MOVE IN ONE GO!
I UNDERSTAND HOW IMPORTANT IT IS TO YOU TO SAVE MONEY...
...BECAUSE I'M THE SAME WAY!

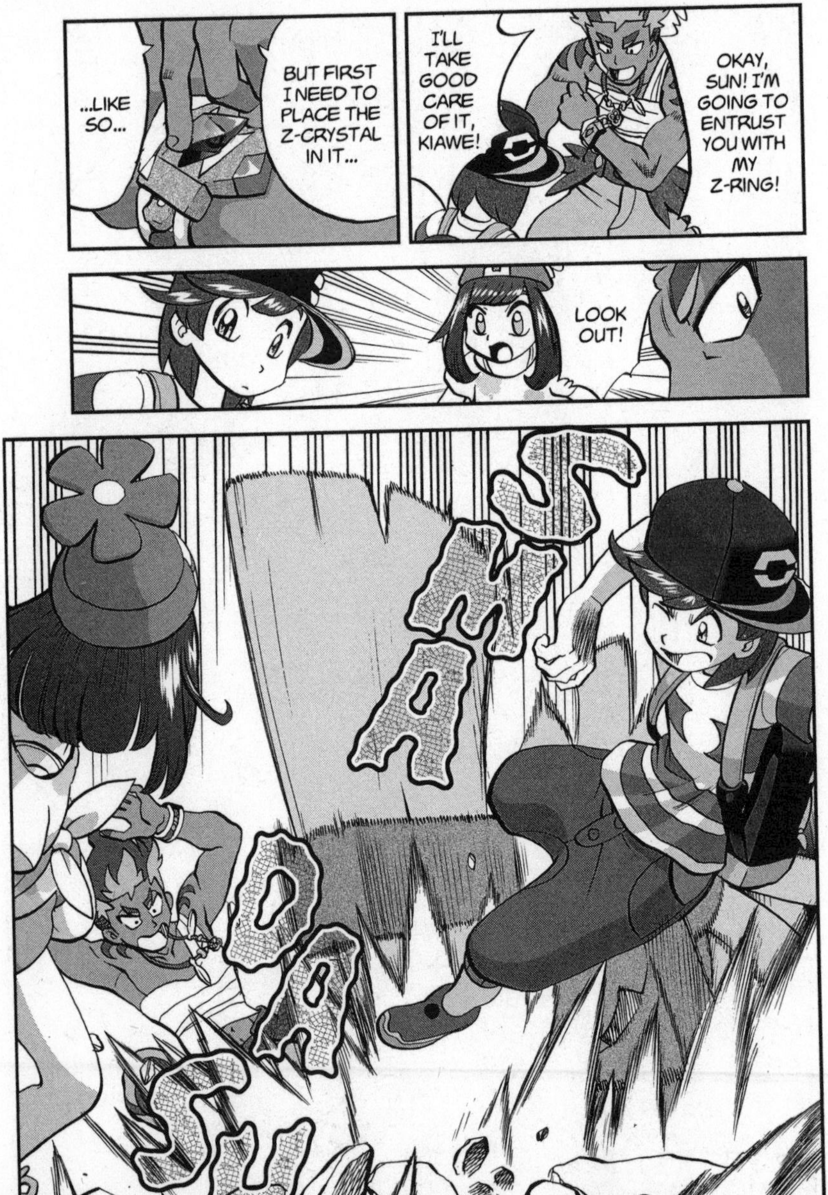
OKAY, SUN! I'M GOING TO ENTRUST YOU WITH MY Z-RING!
I'LL TAKE GOOD CARE OF IT, KIAWE!
BUT FIRST I NEED TO PLACE THE Z-CRYSTAL IN IT...
...LIKE SO...
LOOK OUT!

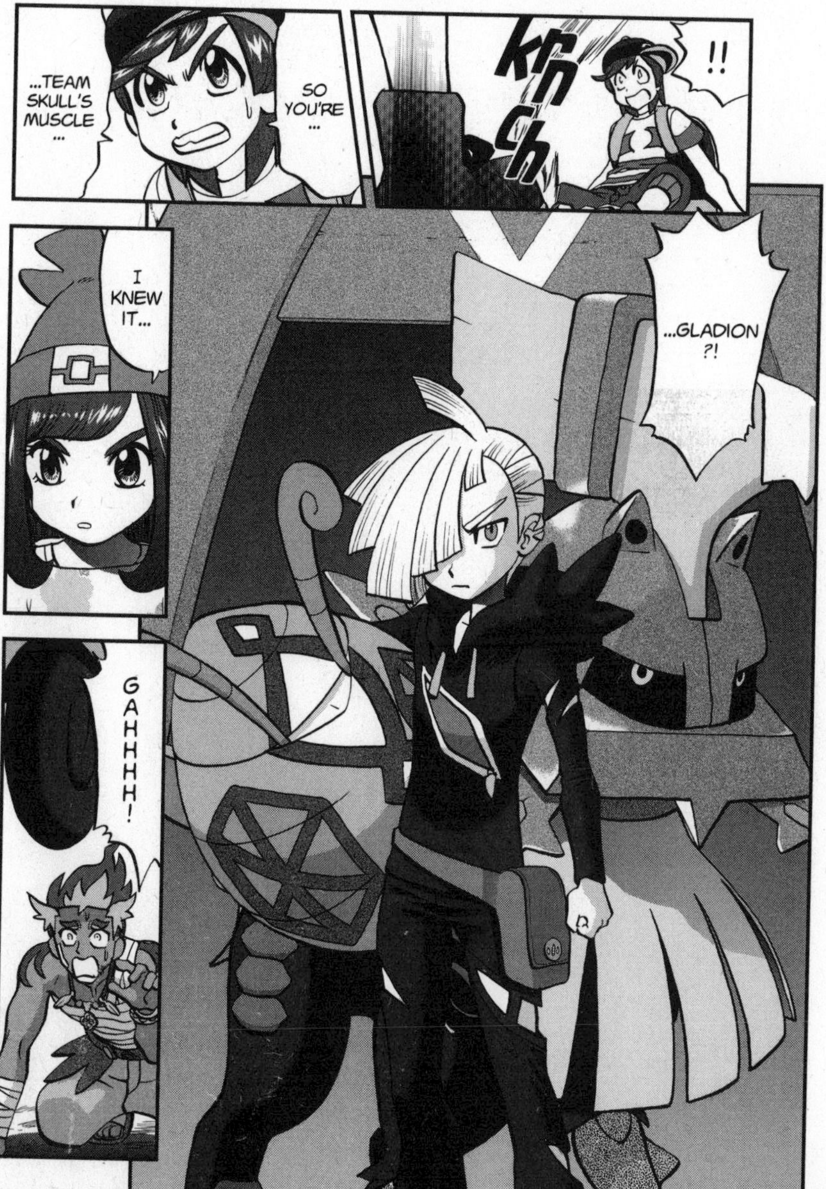
krnch
!!
SO YOU'RE ...
...TEAM SKULL'S MUSCLE ...
...GLADION ?!
I KNEW IT...
GAHHHHH!

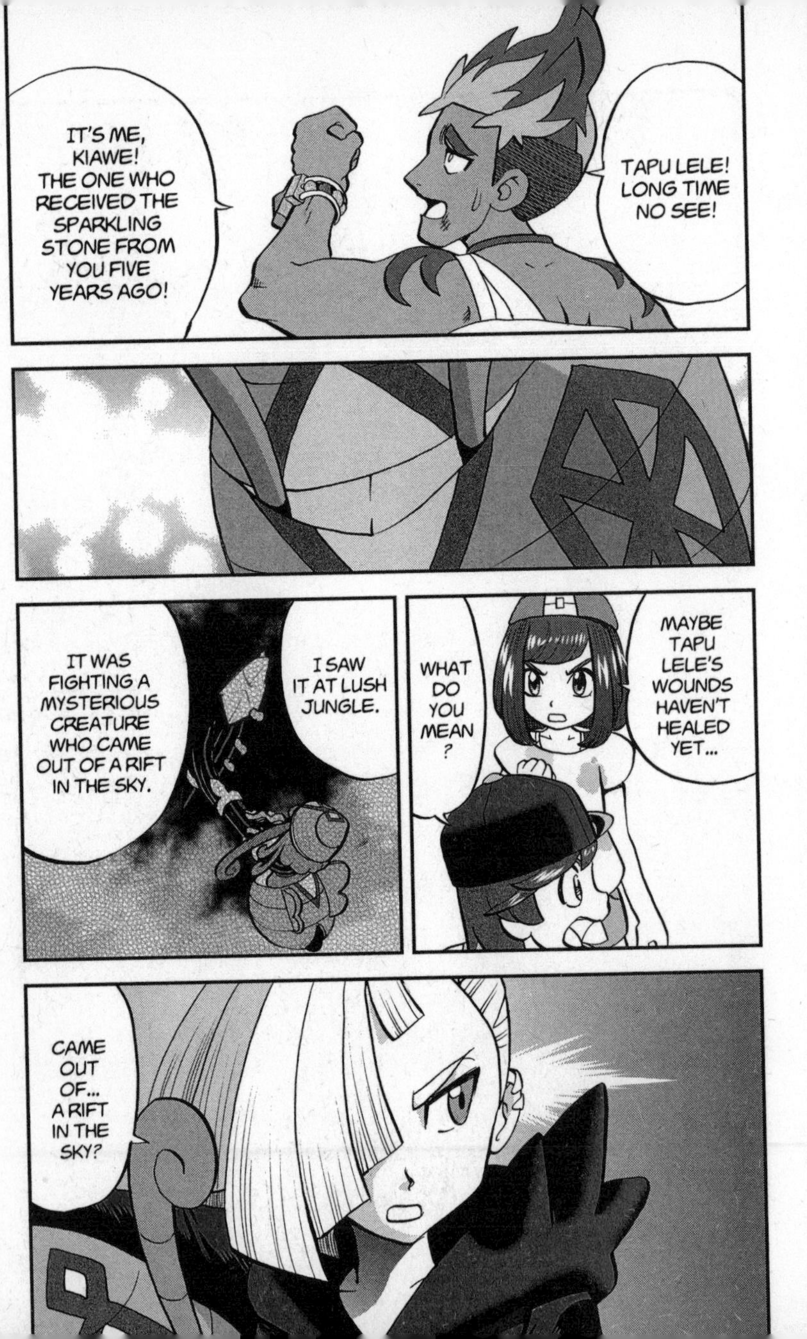
TAPU LELE! LONG TIME NO SEE!
IT'S ME, KIAWE! THE ONE WHO RECEIVED THE SPARKLING STONE FROM YOU FIVE YEARS AGO!
MAYBE TAPU LELE'S WOUNDS HAVEN'T HEALED YET...
WHAT DO YOU MEAN?
I SAW IT AT LUSH JUNGLE.
IT WAS FIGHTING A MYSTERIOUS CREATURE WHO CAME OUT OF A RIFT IN THE SKY.
CAME OUT OF... A RIFT IN THE SKY?

NOW I GET IT...
THE REASON I MANAGED TO CAPTURE IT SO EASILY...
...WAS BECAUSE IT HAD BEEN WEAKENED IN BATTLE AGAINST THEM.
GLA-DION!
WHAT DO YOU WANT?!
YOU SAY YOU WORK FOR TEAM SKULL, BUT...
...WHAT'S YOUR REAL AGENDA?
IT'S ALL...
...TO GET AHOLD OF THE TAPU.
I MISSED MY OPPOR-TUNITY AT MELEMELE BECAUSE OF AN UNEX-PECTED CANDI-DATE.
Wait, is he making fun of me?!
What unexpected candidate...?
LISTEN UP!
A CRISIS IS APPROACHING ALOLA, AND THE TAPU ARE AGITATED BECAUSE THEY SENSE IT COMING.

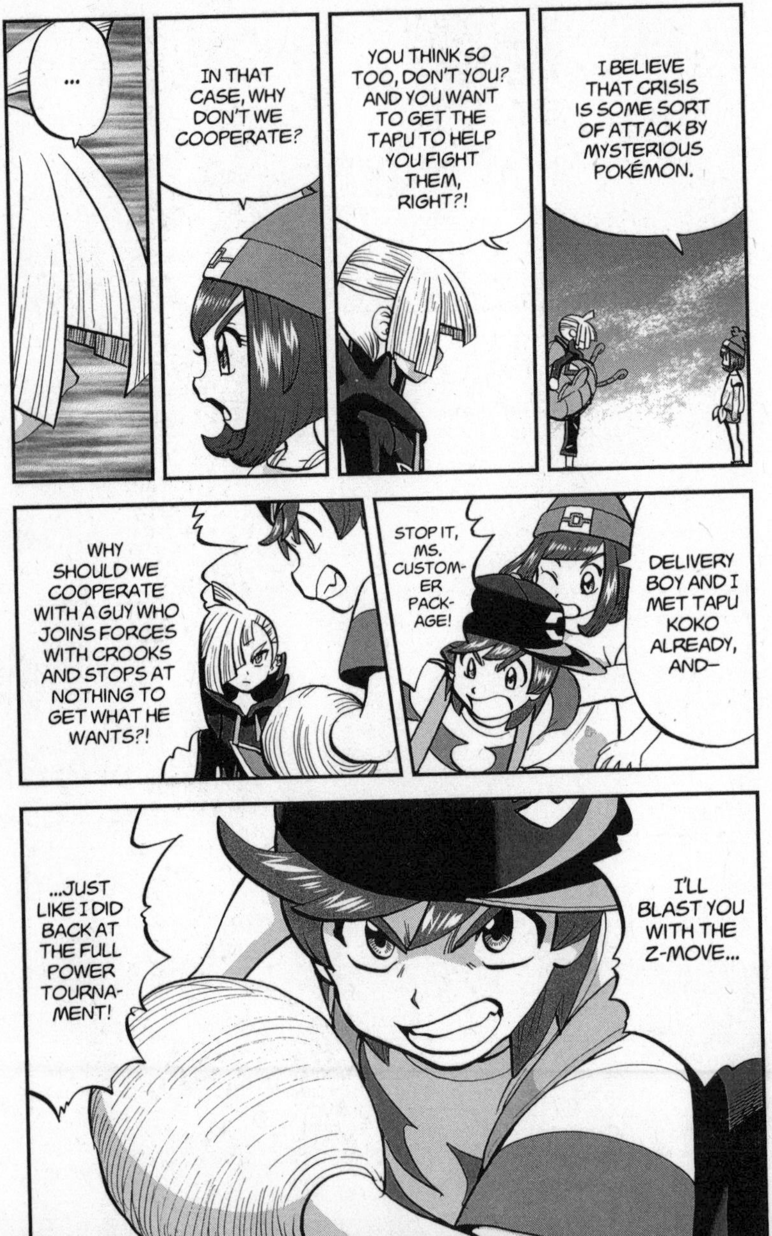
I BELIEVE THAT CRISIS IS SOME SORT OF ATTACK BY MYSTERIOUS POKÉMON.
YOU THINK SO TOO, DON'T YOU? AND YOU WANT TO GET THE TAPU TO HELP YOU FIGHT THEM, RIGHT?!
IN THAT CASE, WHY DON'T WE COOPERATE?
...
DELIVERY BOY AND I MET TAPU KOKO ALREADY, AND–
STOP IT, MS. CUSTOMER-PACKAGE!
WHY SHOULD WE COOPERATE WITH A GUY WHO JOINS FORCES WITH CROOKS AND STOPS AT NOTHING TO GET WHAT HE WANTS?!
I'LL BLAST YOU WITH THE Z-MOVE...
...JUST LIKE I DID BACK AT THE FULL POWER TOURNAMENT!

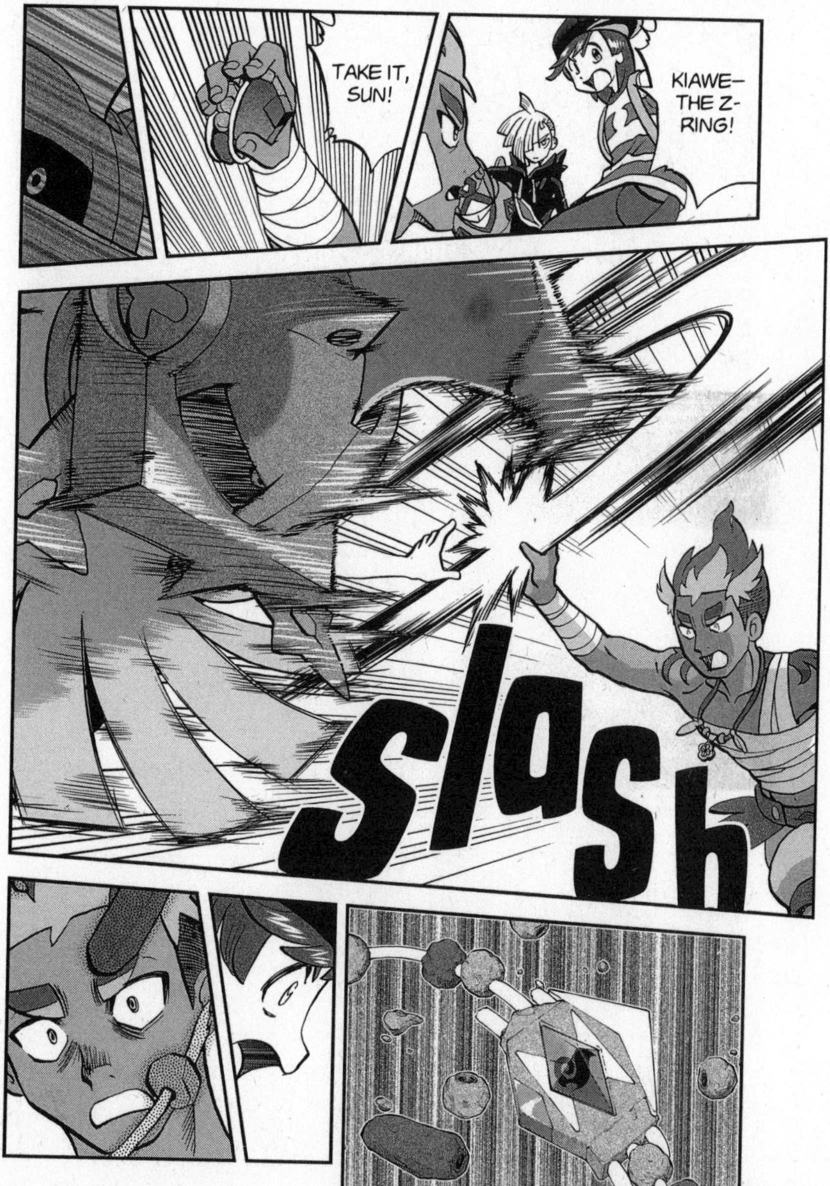
KIAWE—THE Z-RING!
TAKE IT, SUN!
slash

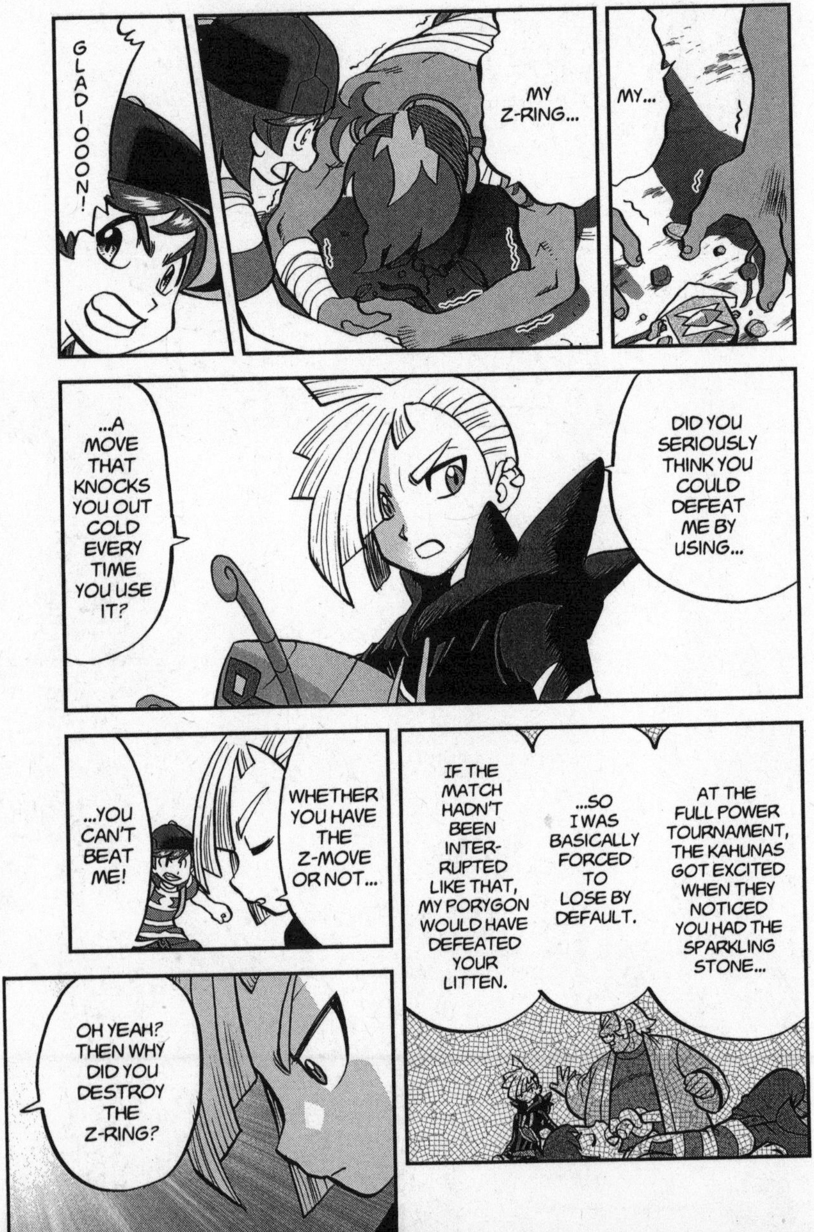
MY...
MY Z-RING...
GLADIOOOON!
DID YOU SERIOUSLY THINK YOU COULD DEFEAT ME BY USING...
...A MOVE THAT KNOCKS YOU OUT COLD EVERY TIME YOU USE IT?
AT THE FULL POWER TOURNAMENT, THE KAHUNAS GOT EXCITED WHEN THEY NOTICED YOU HAD THE SPARKLING STONE...
...SO I WAS BASICALLY FORCED TO LOSE BY DEFAULT.
IF THE MATCH HADN'T BEEN INTER-RUPTED LIKE THAT, MY PORYGON WOULD HAVE DEFEATED YOUR LITTEN.
WHETHER YOU HAVE THE Z-MOVE OR NOT...
...YOU CAN'T BEAT ME!
OH YEAH? THEN WHY DID YOU DESTROY THE Z-RING?

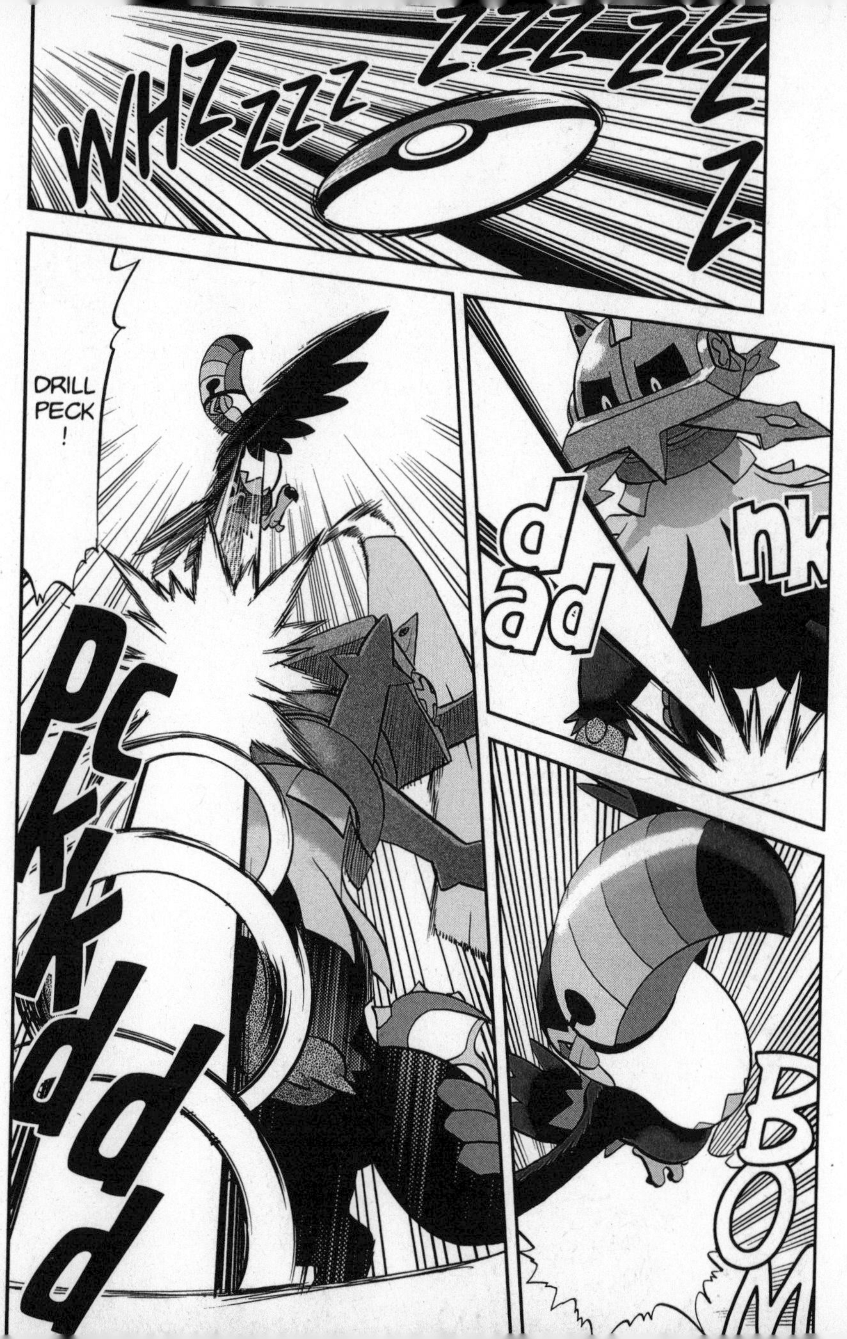
WHZzzzZZZZZZZZZZZ
BOOM
DRILL PECK!

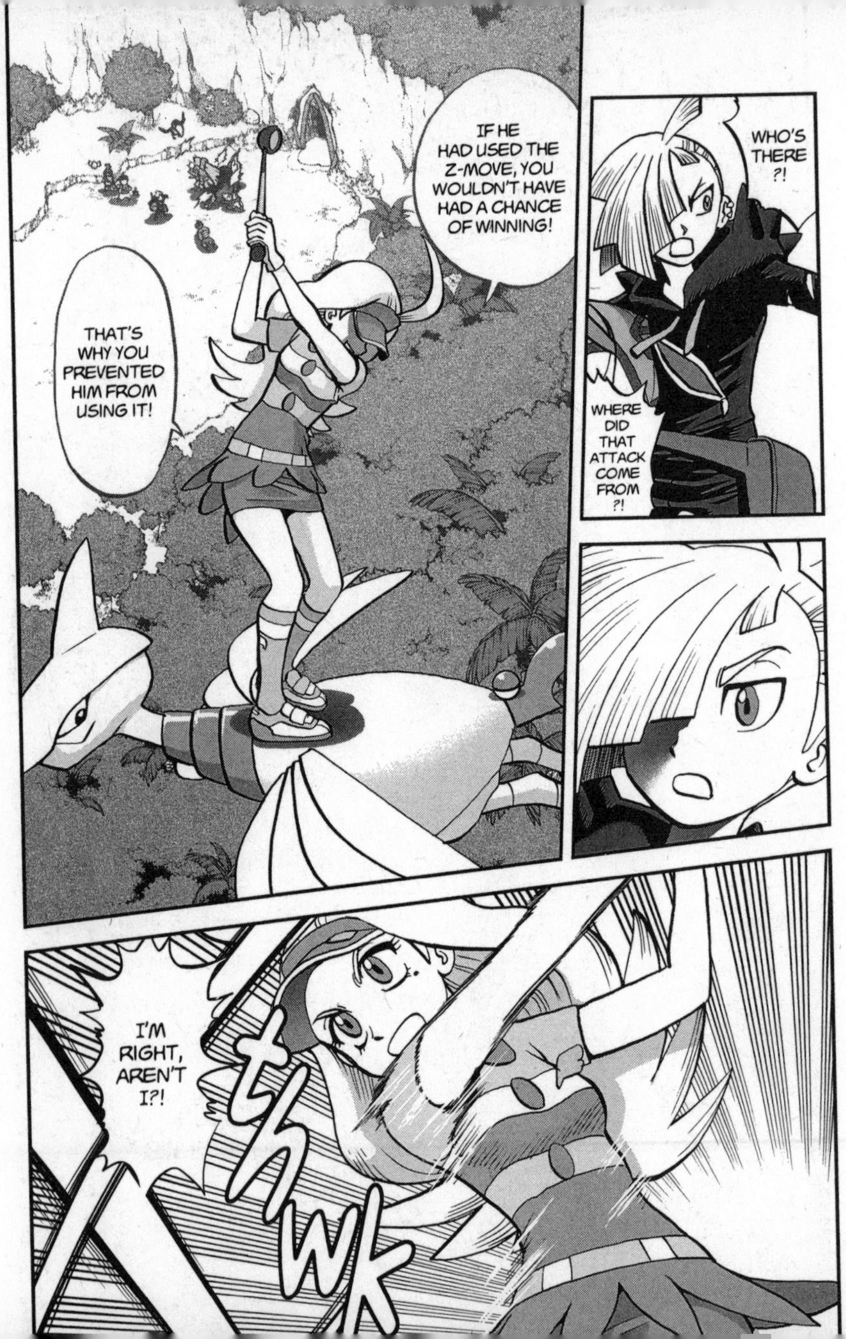
WHO'S THERE ?!
WHERE DID THAT ATTACK COME FROM ?!
IF HE HAD USED THE Z-MOVE, YOU WOULDN'T HAVE HAD A CHANCE OF WINNING!
THAT'S WHY YOU PREVENTED HIM FROM USING IT!
I'M RIGHT, AREN'T I?!
thwk

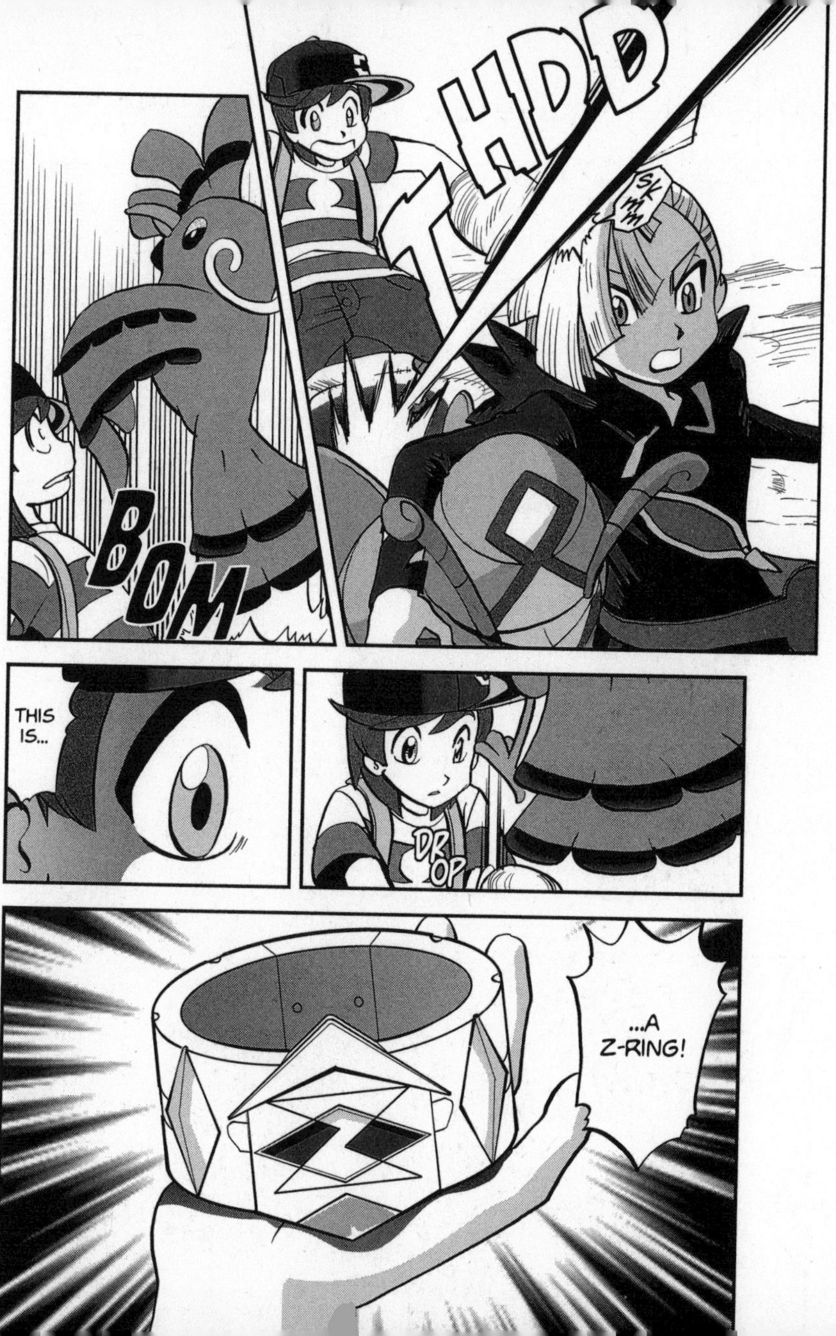
THDD
SKMM
BOM
DROP
THIS IS...
...A Z-RING!

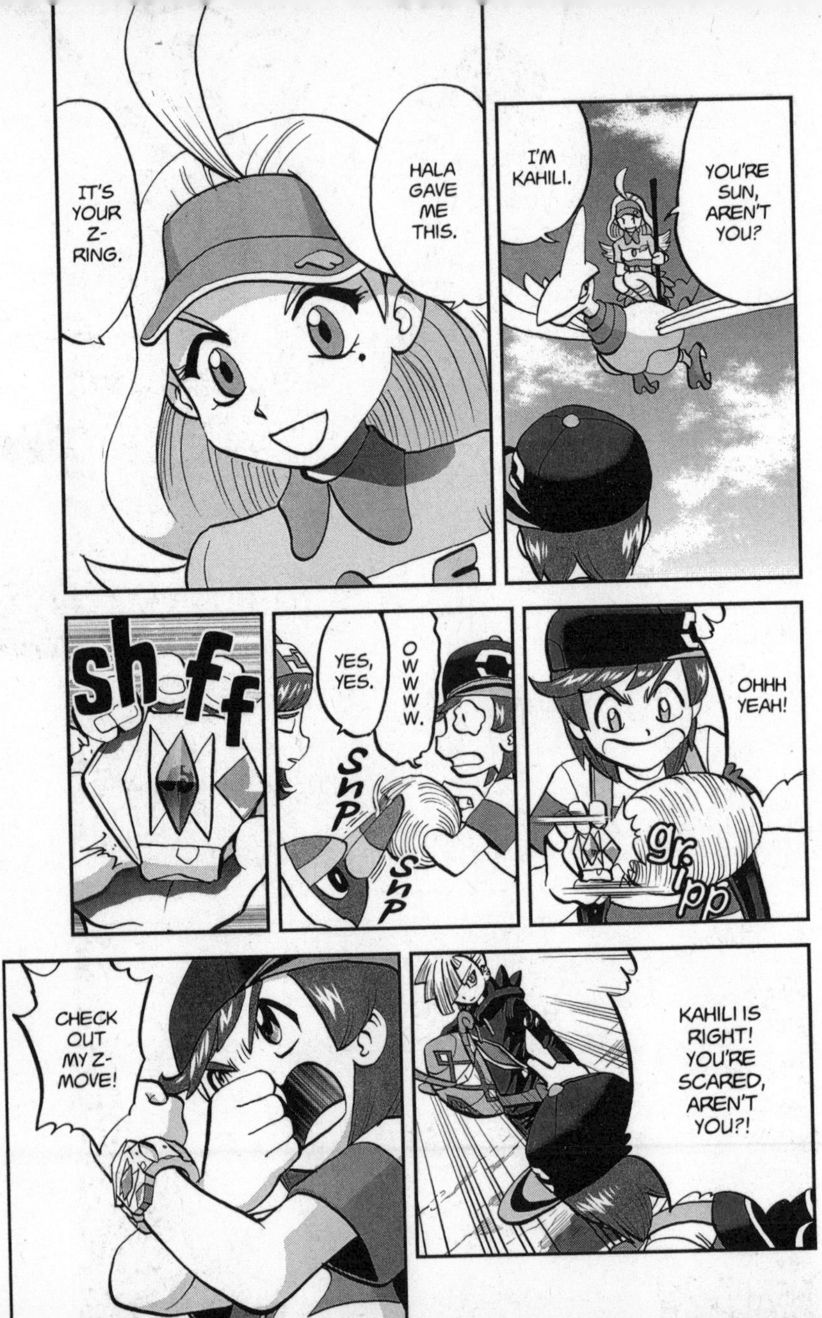
YOU'RE SUN, AREN'T YOU?
I'M KAHILI.
HALA GAVE ME THIS.
IT'S YOUR Z-RING.
OHHH YEAH!
gripp
OWWWW.
YES, YES.
snp
snp
shff
KAHILI IS RIGHT! YOU'RE SCARED, AREN'T YOU?!
CHECK OUT MY Z-MOVE!

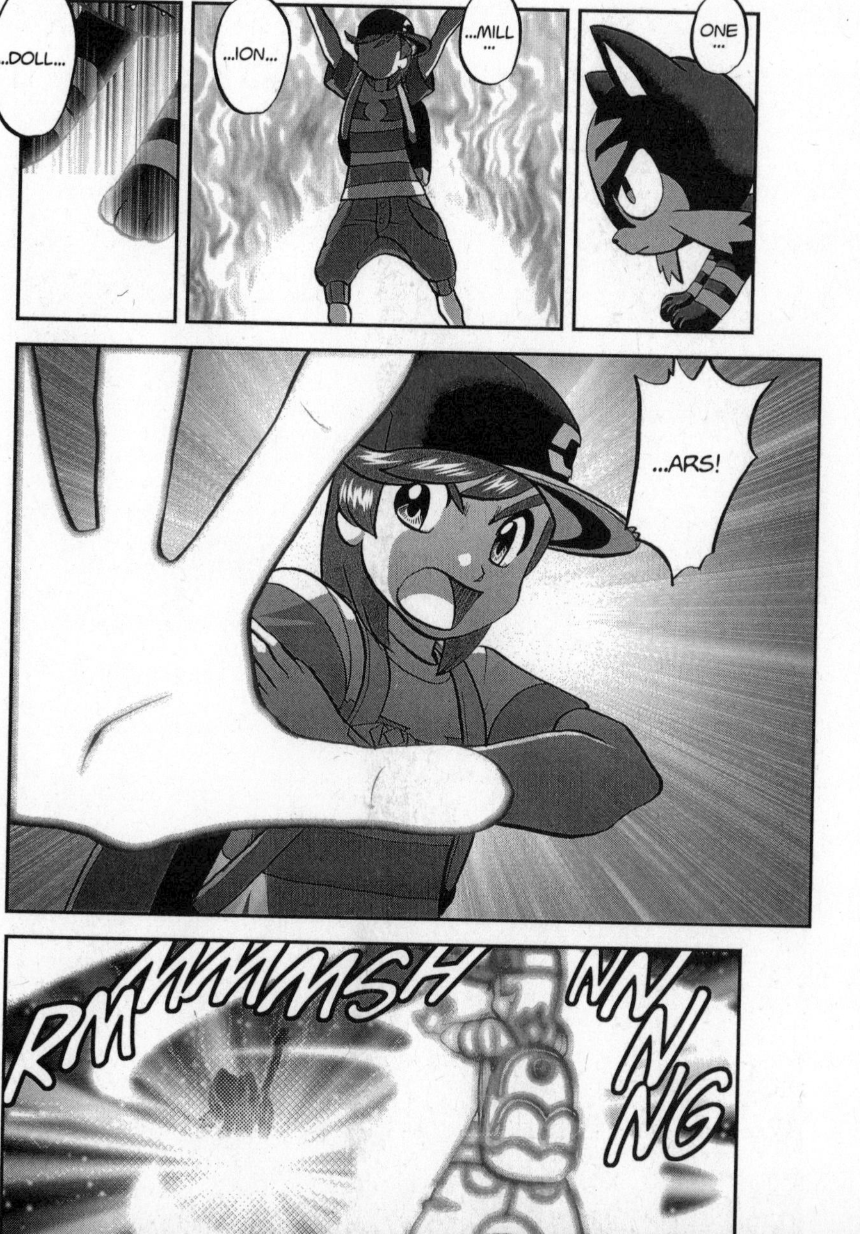
ONE ...
...MILL ...
...ION...
...DOLL...
...ARS!
RMMMMMSHNNNNNG

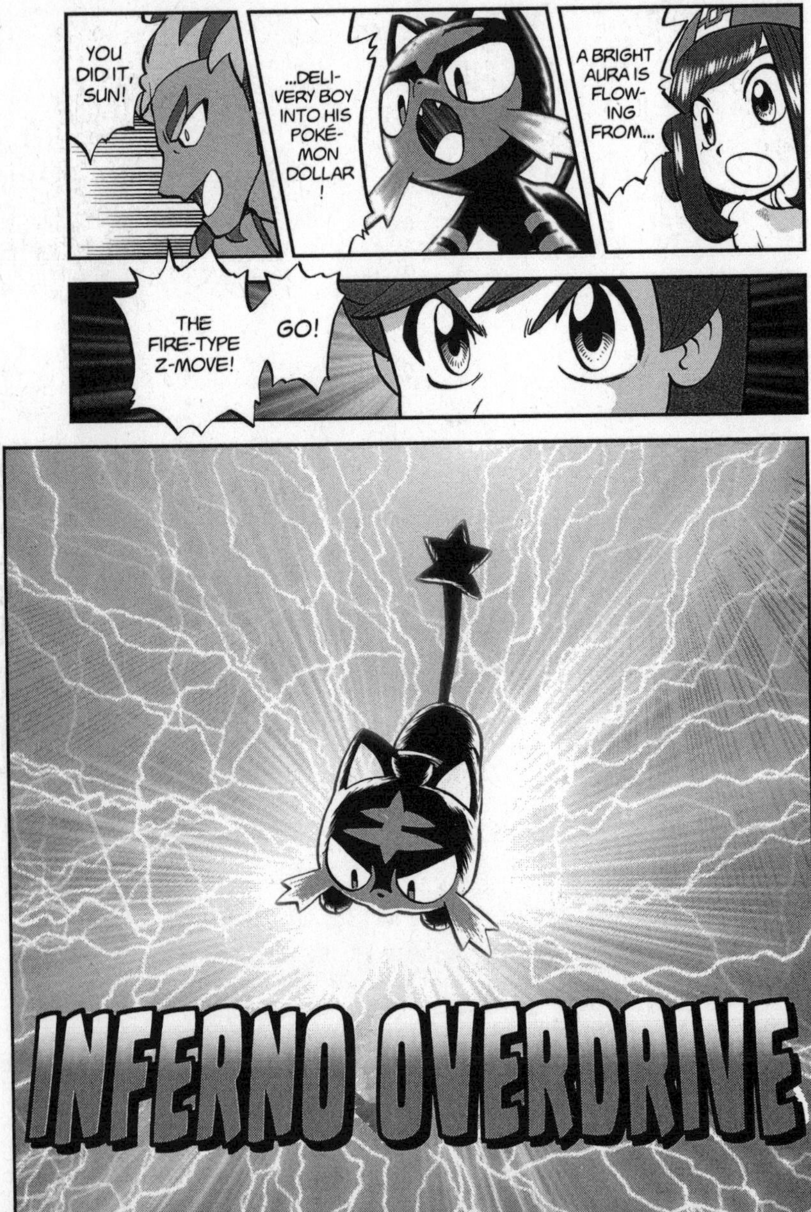
A BRIGHT AURA IS FLOW-ING FROM...
...DELI-VERY BOY INTO HIS POKÉ-MON DOLLAR!
YOU DID IT, SUN!
GO!
THE FIRE-TYPE Z-MOVE!
INFERNO OVERDRIVE

Kahuna

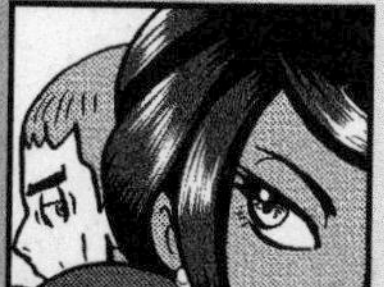

Trainers such as Hala are known for their distinctive personalities. There are Kahunas on Melemele, Akala and Ula'ula, but the Kahuna position of Poni Island is currently empty. Perhaps you'd like to volunteer for it...? (^w^)

Guide to Alola 11

Adventure 13
Unleashing the Incredible Z-Move

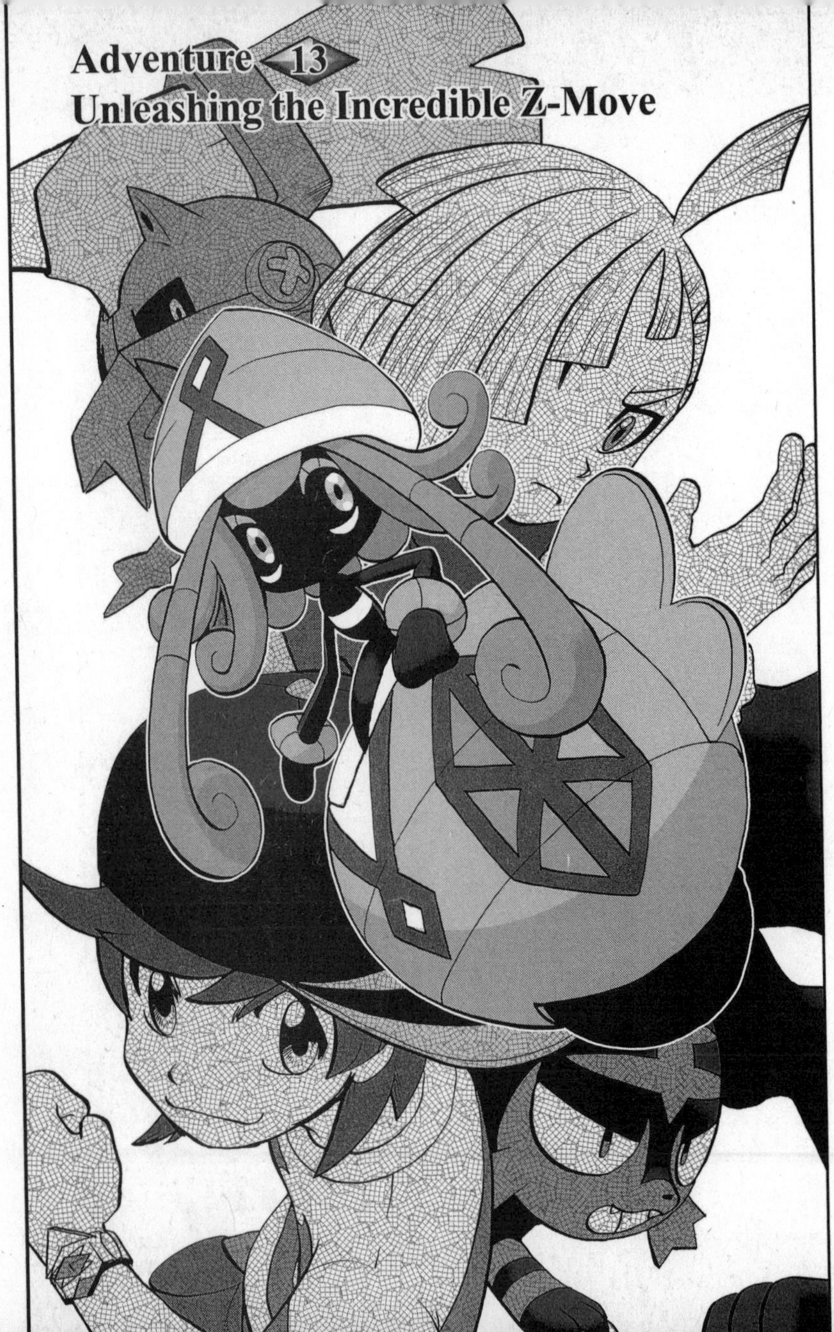

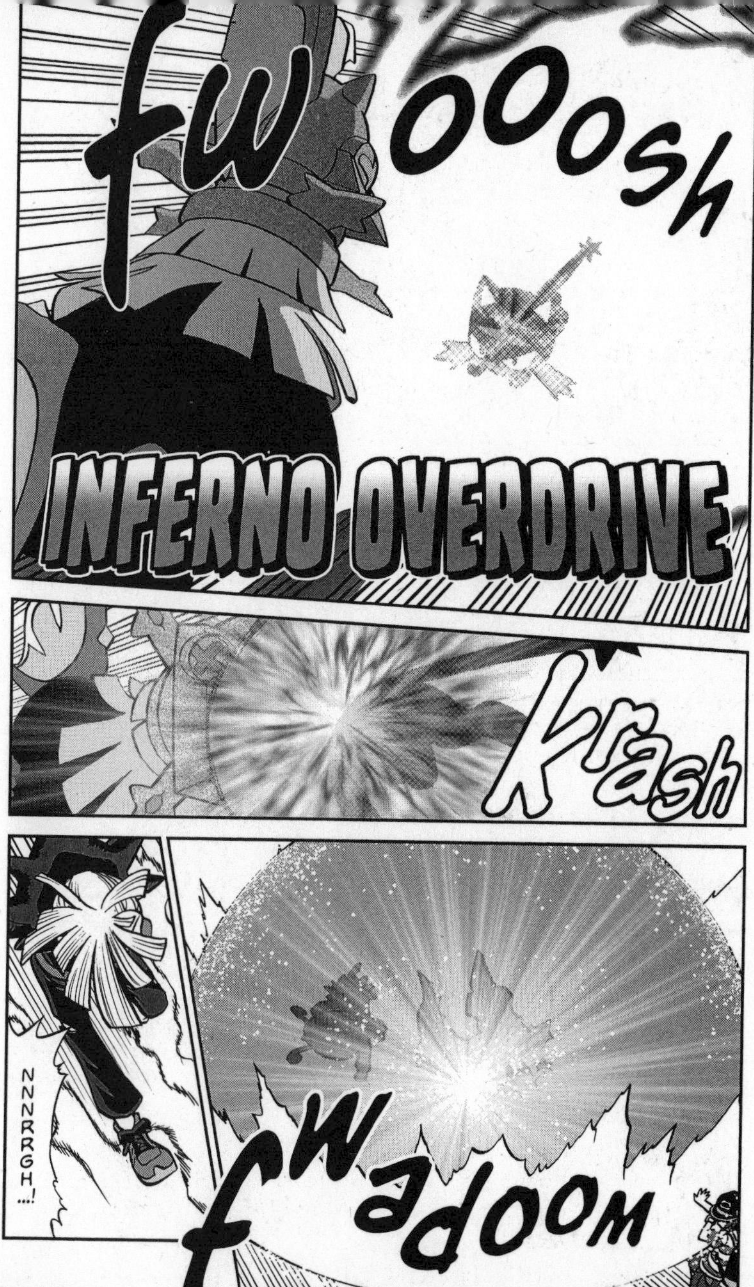
fwoOOosh
INFERNO OVERDRIVE
krash
fwadoom
NNNRRGH...!

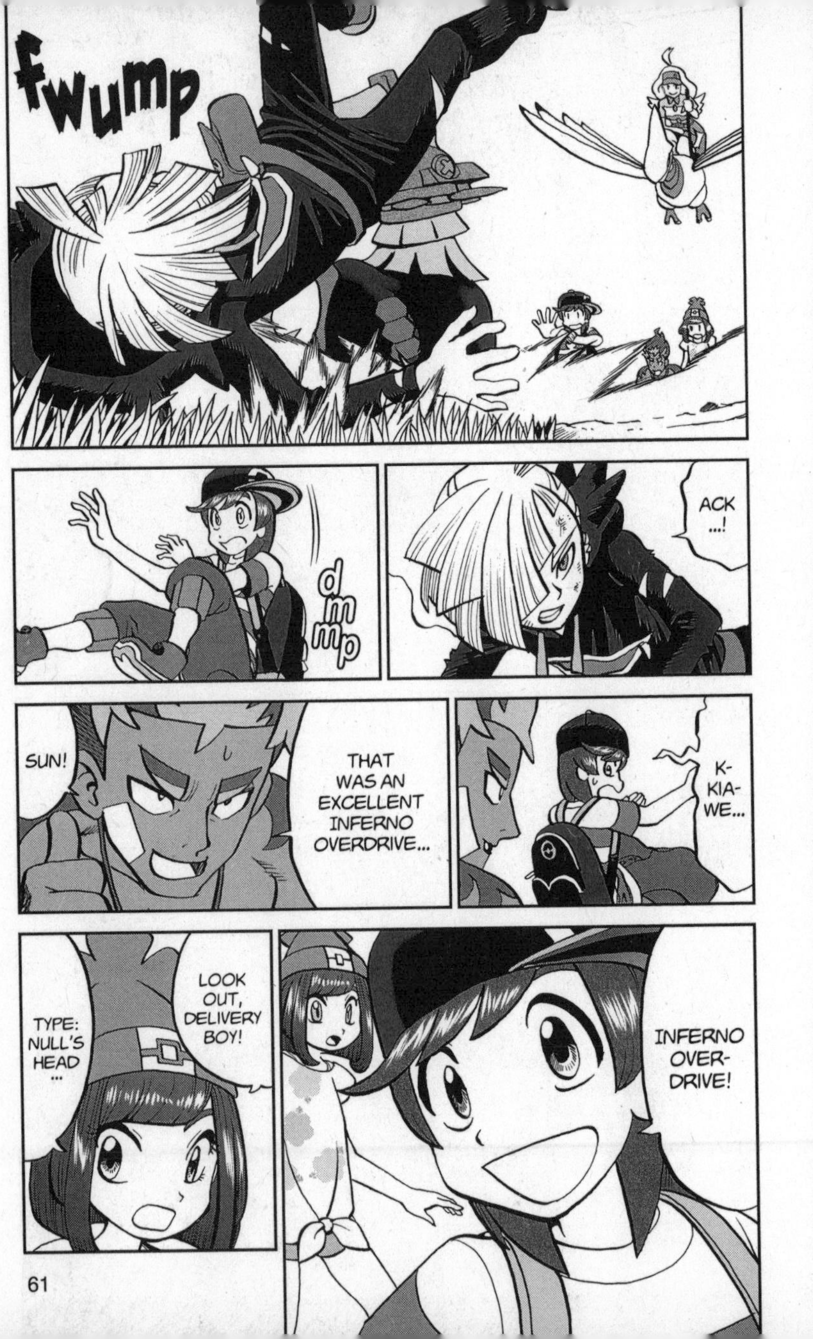
fwump
ACK ...!
dmmp
K-KIA-WE...
SUN!
THAT WAS AN EXCELLENT INFERNO OVERDRIVE...
INFERNO OVER-DRIVE!
LOOK OUT, DELIVERY BOY!
TYPE: NULL'S HEAD ...

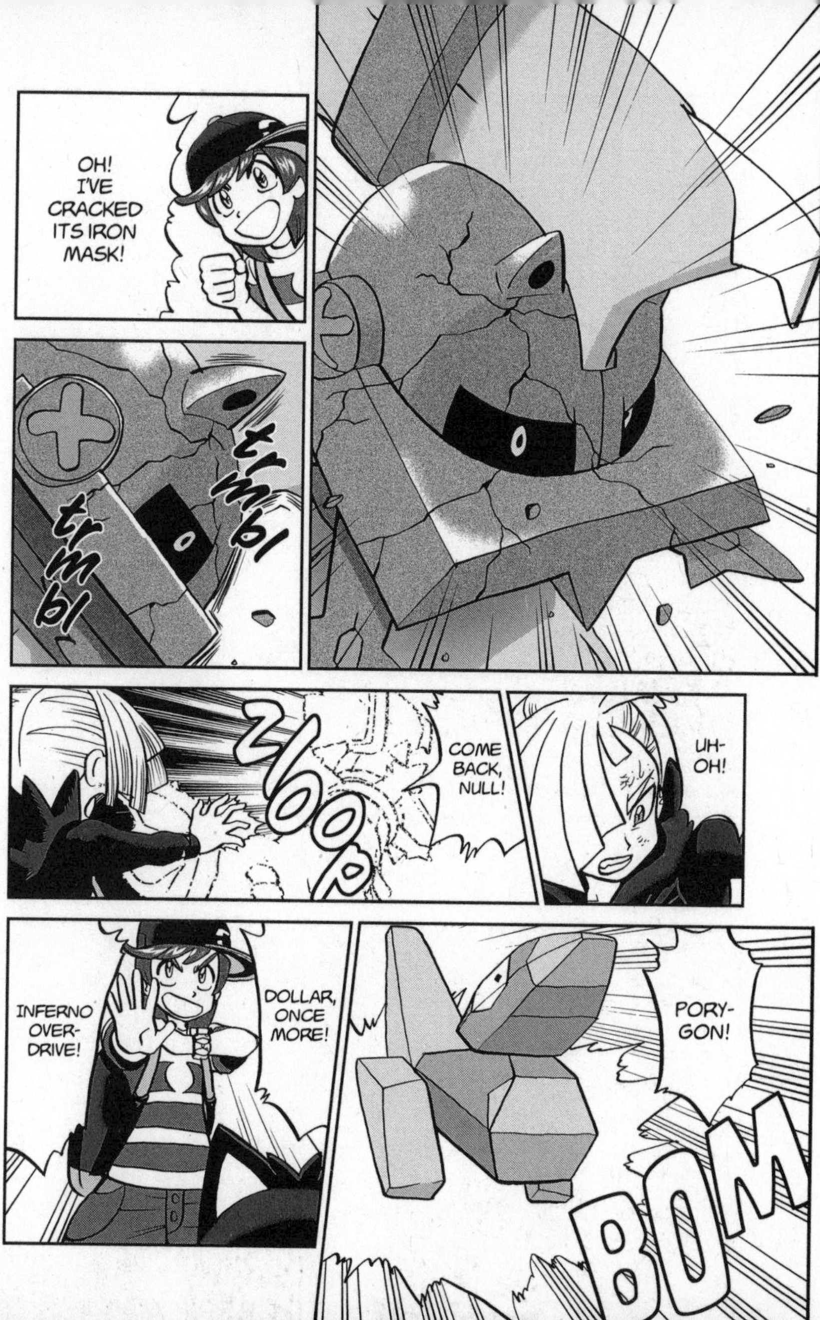
OH! I'VE CRACKED ITS IRON MASK!
trmbl
trmbl
UH-OH!
COME BACK, NULL!
zloop
PORY-GON!
BOM
DOLLAR, ONCE MORE!
INFERNO OVER-DRIVE!

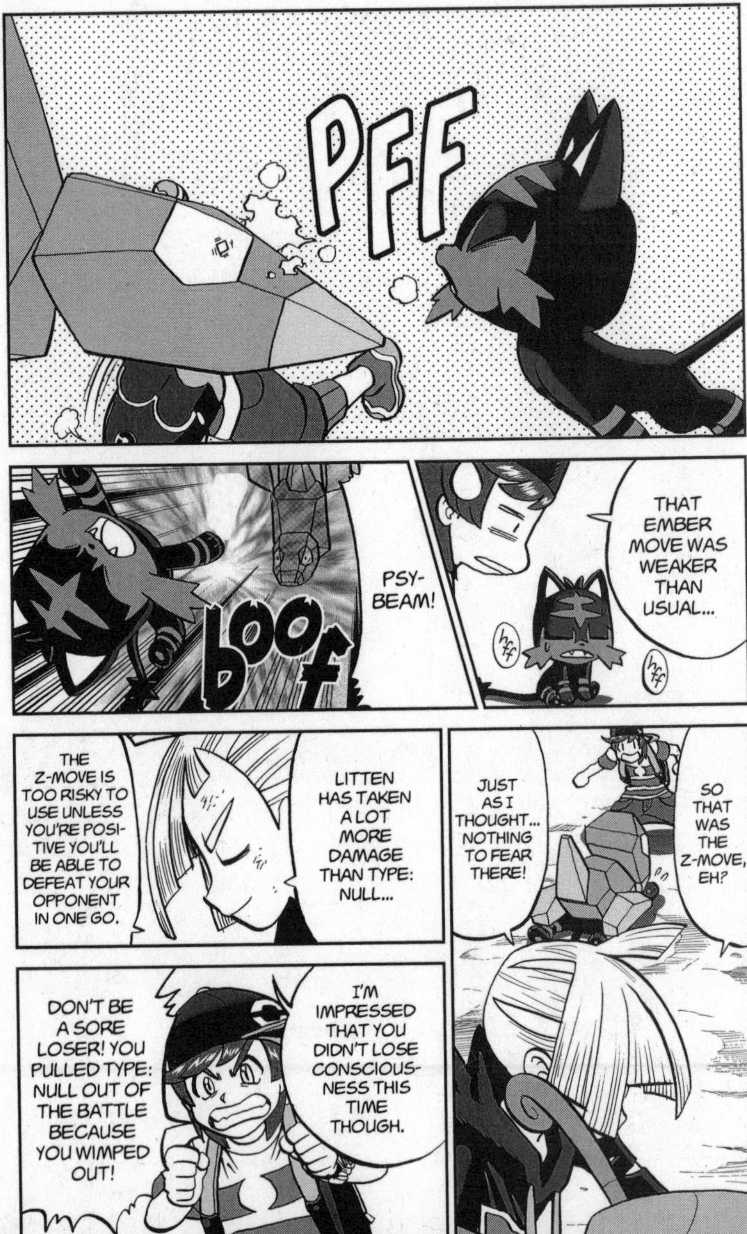
PFF
THAT EMBER MOVE WAS WEAKER THAN USUAL...
hff
hff
PSY-BEAM!
boof
SO THAT WAS THE Z-MOVE, EH?
JUST AS I THOUGHT... NOTHING TO FEAR THERE!
LITTEN HAS TAKEN A LOT MORE DAMAGE THAN TYPE: NULL...
THE Z-MOVE IS TOO RISKY TO USE UNLESS YOU'RE POSITIVE YOU'LL BE ABLE TO DEFEAT YOUR OPPONENT IN ONE GO.
I'M IMPRESSED THAT YOU DIDN'T LOSE CONSCIOUSNESS THIS TIME THOUGH.
DON'T BE A SORE LOSER! YOU PULLED TYPE: NULL OUT OF THE BATTLE BECAUSE YOU WIMPED OUT!

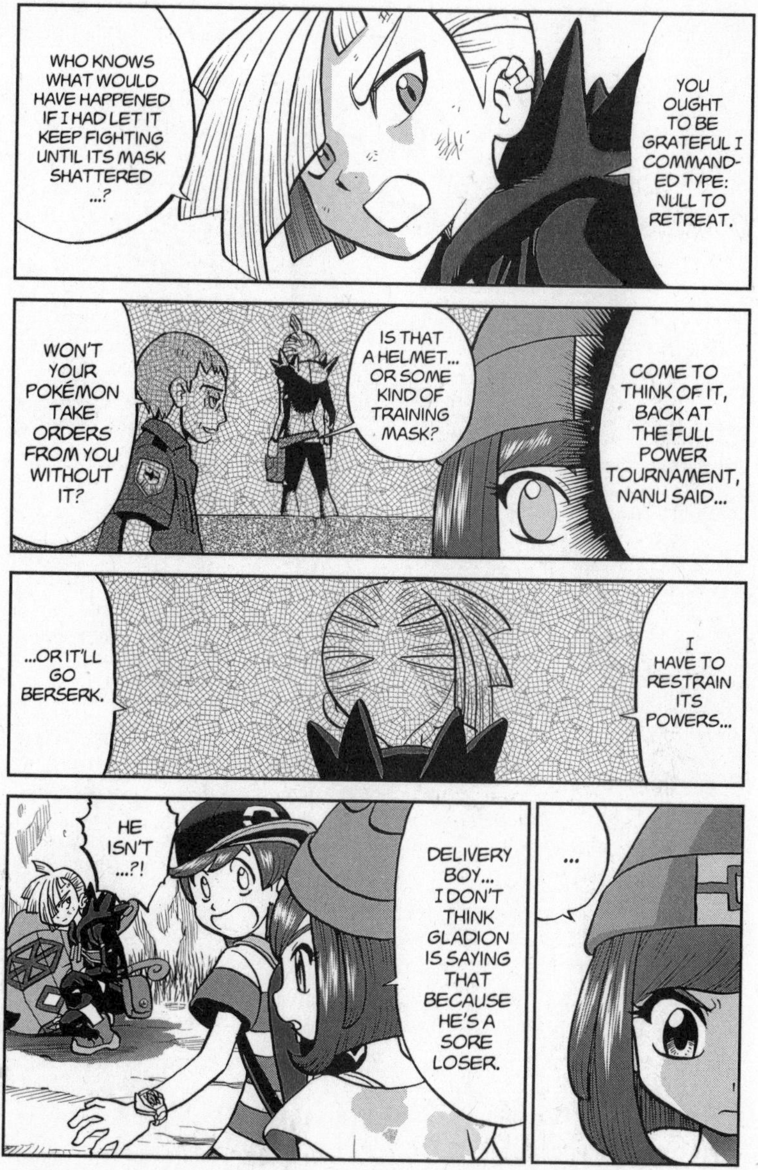
YOU OUGHT TO BE GRATEFUL I COMMANDED TYPE: NULL TO RETREAT.
WHO KNOWS WHAT WOULD HAVE HAPPENED IF I HAD LET IT KEEP FIGHTING UNTIL ITS MASK SHATTERED ...?
COME TO THINK OF IT, BACK AT THE FULL POWER TOURNAMENT, NANU SAID...
IS THAT A HELMET... OR SOME KIND OF TRAINING MASK?
WON'T YOUR POKÉMON TAKE ORDERS FROM YOU WITHOUT IT?
I HAVE TO RESTRAIN ITS POWERS...
...OR IT'LL GO BERSERK.
...
DELIVERY BOY... I DON'T THINK GLADION IS SAYING THAT BECAUSE HE'S A SORE LOSER.
HE ISN'T ...?!

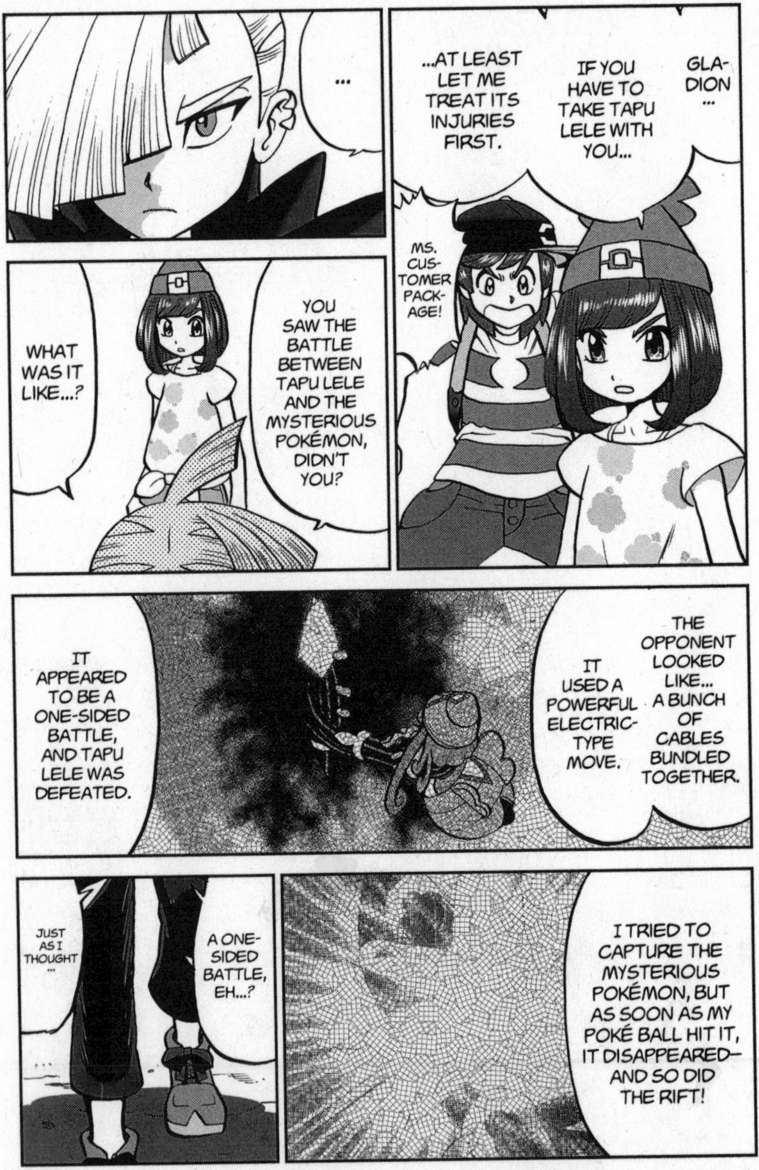
GLADION...
IF YOU HAVE TO TAKE TAPU LELE WITH YOU...
...AT LEAST LET ME TREAT ITS INJURIES FIRST.
MS. CUSTOMER PACKAGE!
...
YOU SAW THE BATTLE BETWEEN TAPU LELE AND THE MYSTERIOUS POKÉMON, DIDN'T YOU?
WHAT WAS IT LIKE...?
THE OPPONENT LOOKED LIKE... A BUNCH OF CABLES BUNDLED TOGETHER.
IT USED A POWERFUL ELECTRIC-TYPE MOVE.
IT APPEARED TO BE A ONE-SIDED BATTLE, AND TAPU LELE WAS DEFEATED.
I TRIED TO CAPTURE THE MYSTERIOUS POKÉMON, BUT AS SOON AS MY POKÉ BALL HIT IT, IT DISAPPEARED—AND SO DID THE RIFT!
A ONE-SIDED BATTLE, EH...?
JUST AS I THOUGHT...
...

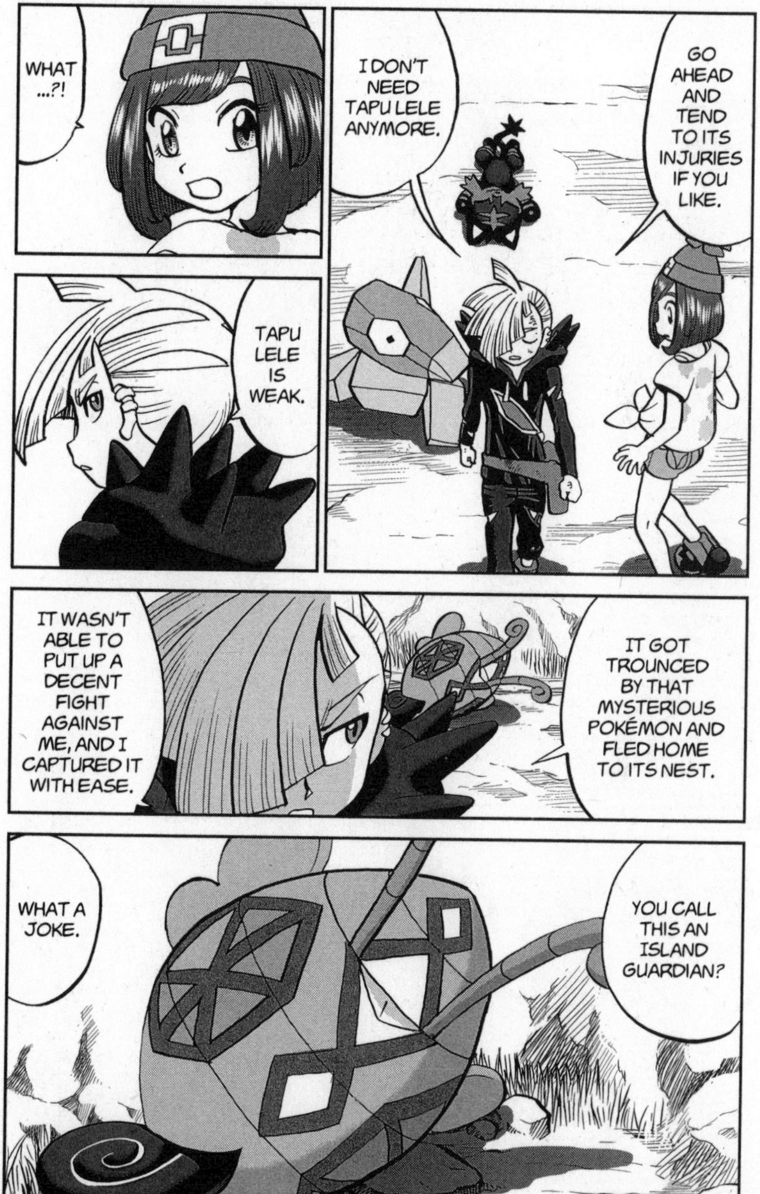
GO AHEAD AND TEND TO ITS INJURIES IF YOU LIKE.
I DON'T NEED TAPU LELE ANYMORE.
WHAT ...?!
TAPU LELE IS WEAK.
IT GOT TROUNCED BY THAT MYSTERIOUS POKÉMON AND FLED HOME TO ITS NEST.
IT WASN'T ABLE TO PUT UP A DECENT FIGHT AGAINST ME, AND I CAPTURED IT WITH EASE.
YOU CALL THIS AN ISLAND GUARDIAN?
WHAT A JOKE.

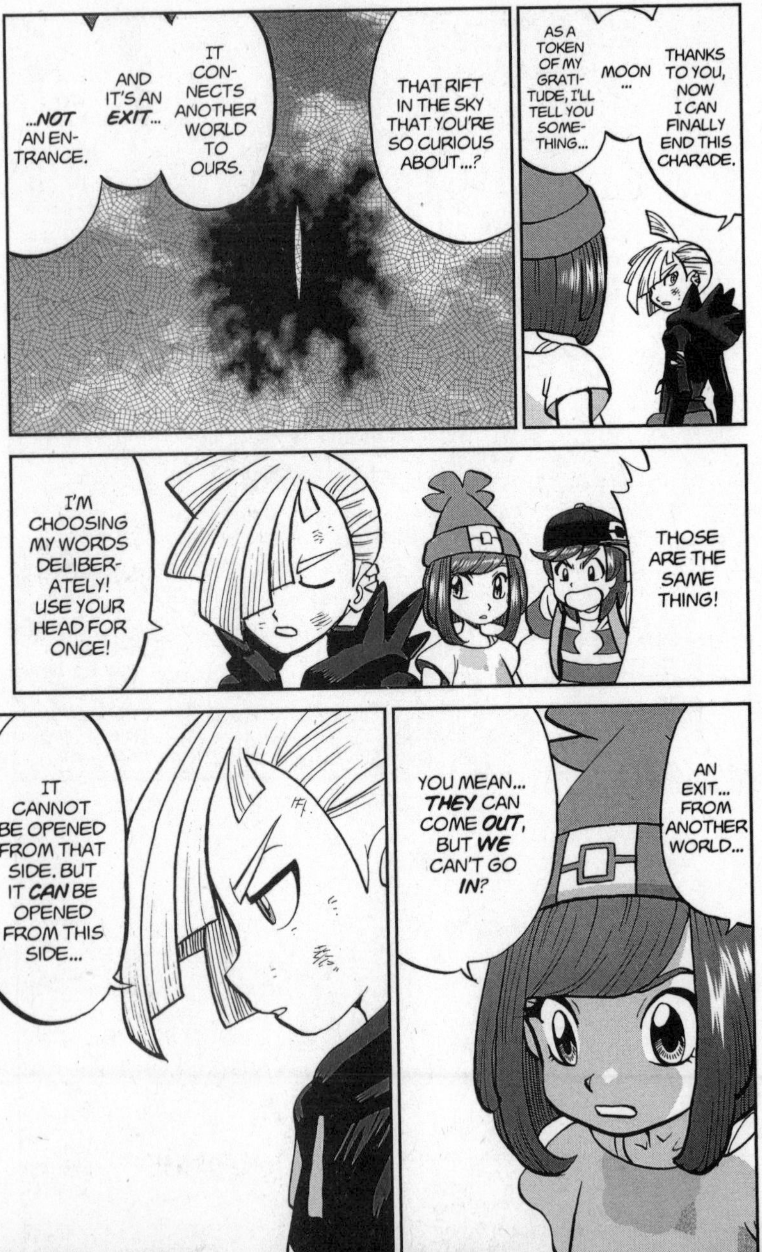
THANKS TO YOU, NOW I CAN FINALLY END THIS CHARADE.
MOON ...
AS A TOKEN OF MY GRATITUDE, I'LL TELL YOU SOMETHING...
THAT RIFT IN THE SKY THAT YOU'RE SO CURIOUS ABOUT...?
IT CONNECTS ANOTHER WORLD TO OURS.
AND IT'S AN EXIT...
...NOT AN ENTRANCE.
THOSE ARE THE SAME THING!
I'M CHOOSING MY WORDS DELIBERATELY! USE YOUR HEAD FOR ONCE!
AN EXIT... FROM ANOTHER WORLD...
YOU MEAN... THEY CAN COME OUT, BUT WE CAN'T GO IN?
IT CANNOT BE OPENED FROM THAT SIDE. BUT IT CAN BE OPENED FROM THIS SIDE...

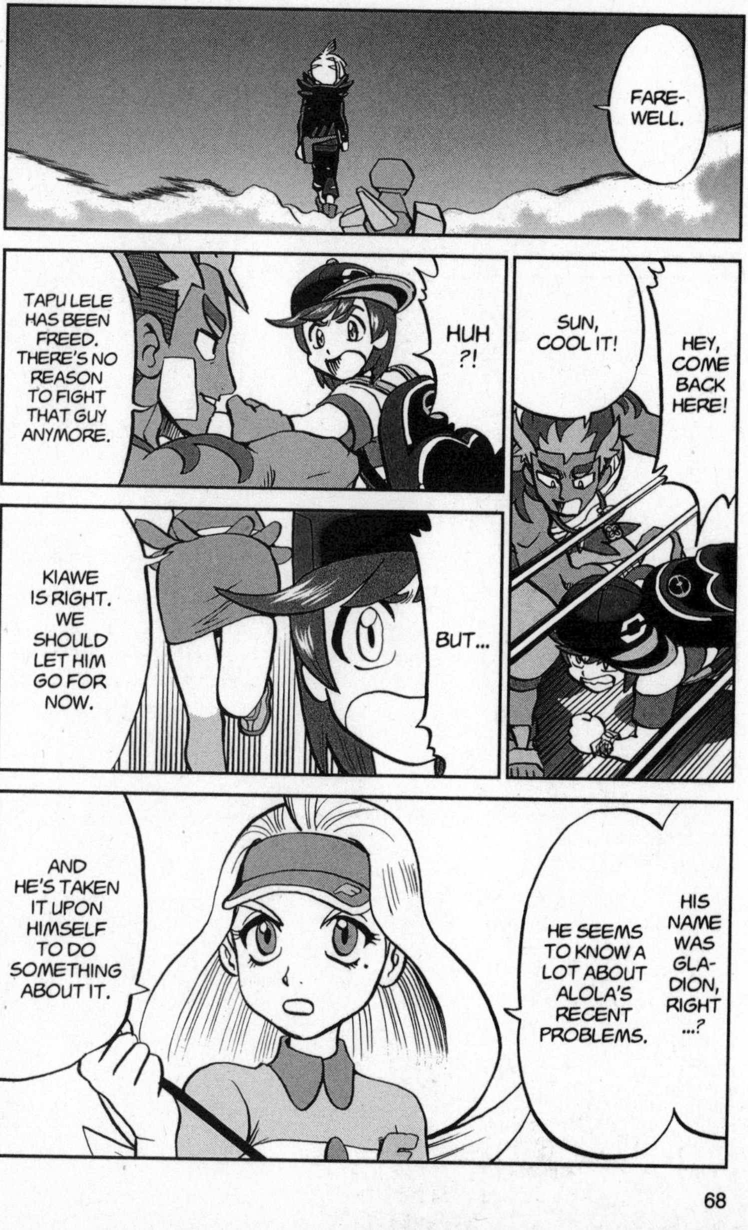
FARE-WELL.
HEY, COME BACK HERE!
SUN, COOL IT!
HUH?!
TAPU LELE HAS BEEN FREED. THERE'S NO REASON TO FIGHT THAT GUY ANYMORE.
BUT...
KIAWE IS RIGHT. WE SHOULD LET HIM GO FOR NOW.
HIS NAME WAS GLA-DION, RIGHT...?
HE SEEMS TO KNOW A LOT ABOUT ALOLA'S RECENT PROBLEMS.
AND HE'S TAKEN IT UPON HIMSELF TO DO SOMETHING ABOUT IT.

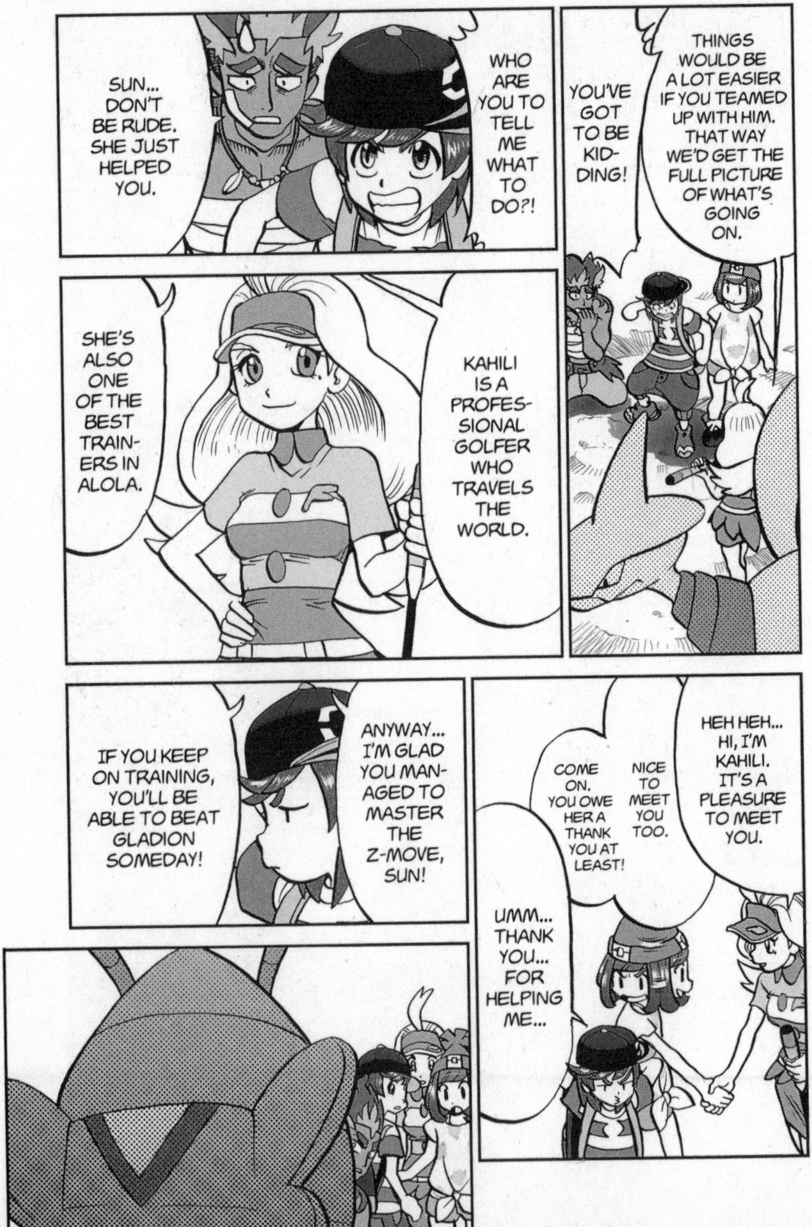
THINGS WOULD BE A LOT EASIER IF YOU TEAMED UP WITH HIM. THAT WAY WE'D GET THE FULL PICTURE OF WHAT'S GOING ON.
YOU'VE GOT TO BE KID-DING!
WHO ARE YOU TO TELL ME WHAT TO DO?!
SUN... DON'T BE RUDE. SHE JUST HELPED YOU.
KAHILI IS A PROFES-SIONAL GOLFER WHO TRAVELS THE WORLD.
SHE'S ALSO ONE OF THE BEST TRAIN-ERS IN ALOLA.
HEH HEH... HI, I'M KAHILI. IT'S A PLEASURE TO MEET YOU.
NICE TO MEET YOU TOO.
COME ON. YOU OWE HER A THANK YOU AT LEAST!
UMM... THANK YOU... FOR HELPING ME...
ANYWAY... I'M GLAD YOU MAN-AGED TO MASTER THE Z-MOVE, SUN!
IF YOU KEEP ON TRAINING, YOU'LL BE ABLE TO BEAT GLADION SOMEDAY!

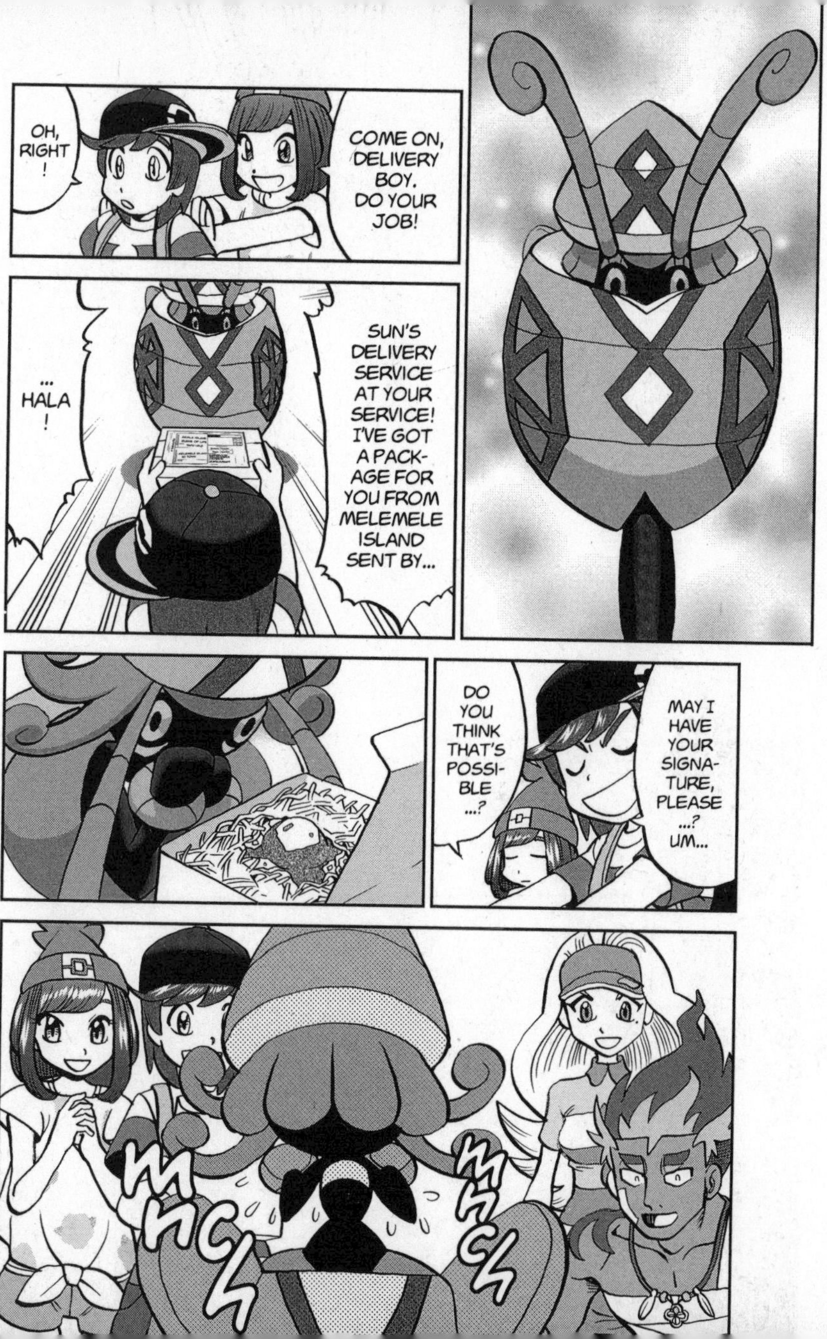
COME ON, DELIVERY BOY. DO YOUR JOB!
OH, RIGHT!
SUN'S DELIVERY SERVICE AT YOUR SERVICE! I'VE GOT A PACKAGE FOR YOU FROM MELEMELE ISLAND SENT BY...
...HALA!
MAY I HAVE YOUR SIGNATURE, PLEASE...? UM...
DO YOU THINK THAT'S POSSIBLE...?
MNCH
MNCH

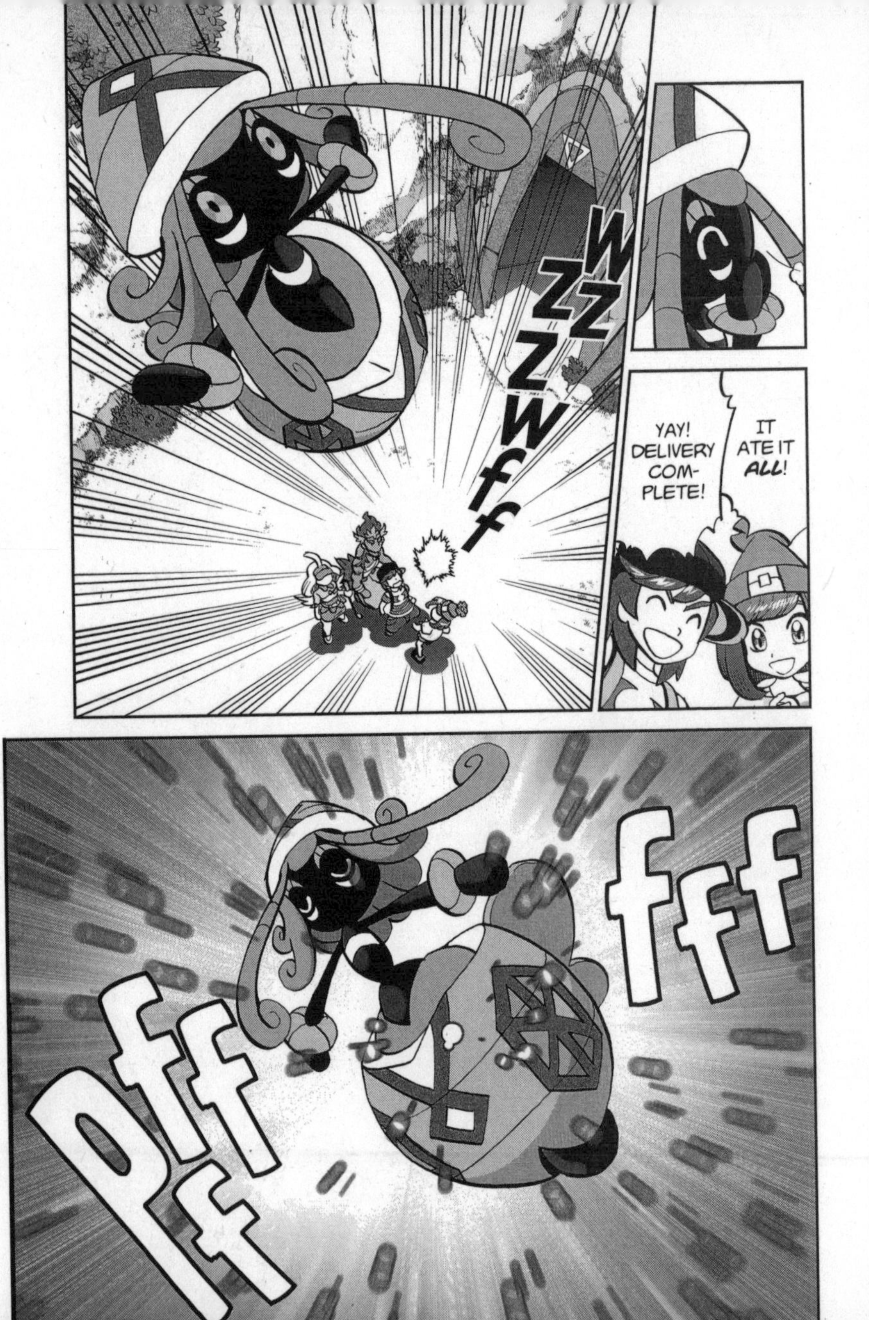
IT ATE IT ALL!
YAY! DELIVERY COM-PLETE!
WZZZZWff
fff
Pfff

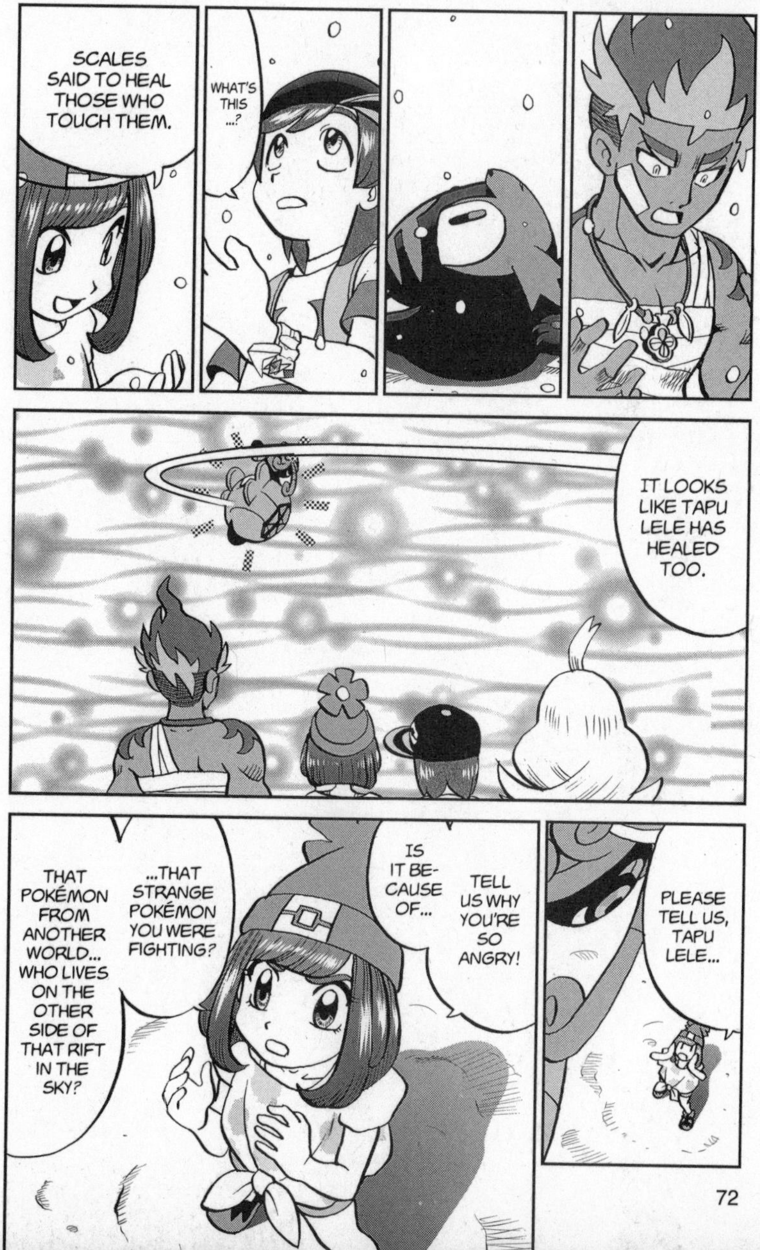
WHAT'S THIS ...?
SCALES SAID TO HEAL THOSE WHO TOUCH THEM.
IT LOOKS LIKE TAPU LELE HAS HEALED TOO.
PLEASE TELL US, TAPU LELE...
TELL US WHY YOU'RE SO ANGRY!
IS IT BE-CAUSE OF...
...THAT STRANGE POKÉMON YOU WERE FIGHTING?
THAT POKÉMON FROM ANOTHER WORLD... WHO LIVES ON THE OTHER SIDE OF THAT RIFT IN THE SKY?

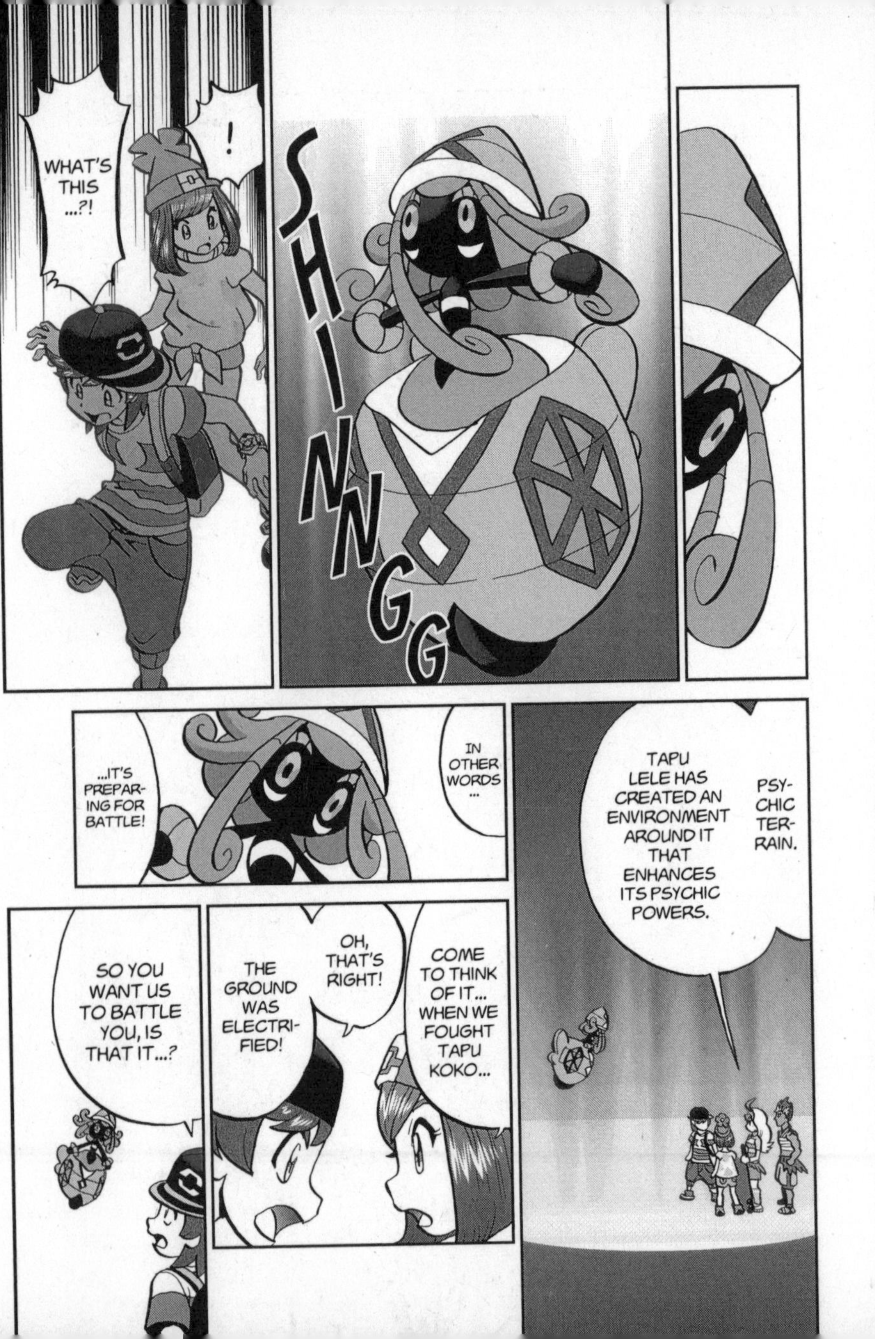
SHINNGG
!
WHAT'S THIS ...?!
PSYCHIC TERRAIN.
TAPU LELE HAS CREATED AN ENVIRONMENT AROUND IT THAT ENHANCES ITS PSYCHIC POWERS.
IN OTHER WORDS ...
...IT'S PREPARING FOR BATTLE!
COME TO THINK OF IT... WHEN WE FOUGHT TAPU KOKO...
OH, THAT'S RIGHT!
THE GROUND WAS ELECTRIFIED!
SO YOU WANT US TO BATTLE YOU, IS THAT IT...?

THE FOUR TAPU—INCLUDING TAPU LELE—ARE NOT THE ISLAND GUARDIANS OF THE PEOPLE OF ALOLA.
THEY ARE IN FACT THE GUARDIANS OF THE OCEAN, EARTH AND SKY OF ALOLA AND ALL WHO LIVE HERE.
THEY ARE INNOCENTS...
...WHO MAY BEHAVE ERRATICALLY AND BE HOSTILE TO HUMANS AT TIMES.
IF YOU WANT TO PREPARE FOR A CRISIS IN ALOLA, IT DOESN'T MATTER WHETHER YOU'RE HUMAN OR POKÉMON...
THE IMPORTANT THING IS THAT YOU HAVE THE POWER TO FIGHT ALONGSIDE THE TAPU.
SO... TAPU LELE WANTS TO TEST US? IS THAT IT?
PROBABLY.
POKÉMON BATTLES CAN ALSO BE A WAY TO REACH OUT AND FORGE A CONNECTION BETWEEN PEOPLE AND POKÉMON.
AS TRAINERS, YOU BOTH UNDERSTAND THAT, DON'T YOU?
SO DON'T HOLD BACK!
GIVE IT EVERYTHING YOU'VE GOT...
...AS IF YOU ARE SINCERELY TRYING TO DEFEAT TAPU LELE!

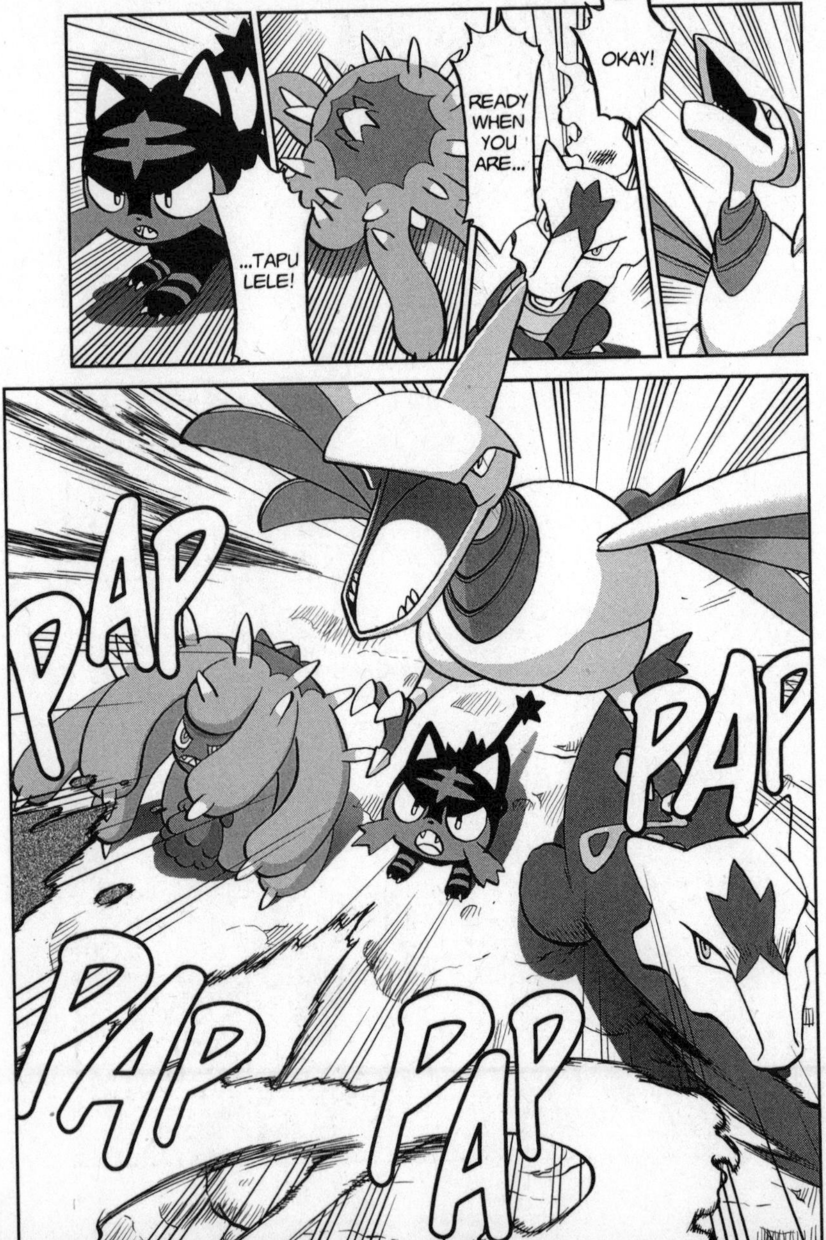
OKAY!
READY WHEN YOU ARE...
...TAPU LELE!
PAP
PAP
PAP
PAP

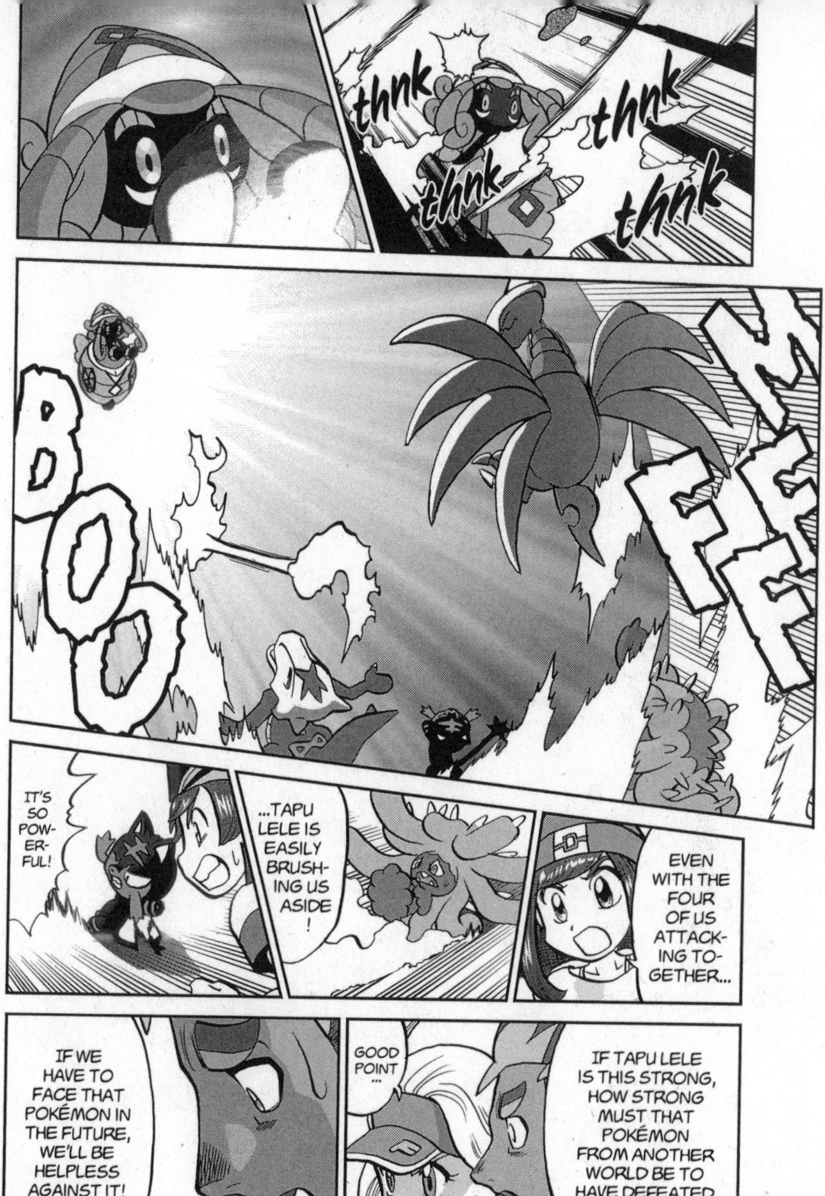
thnk
thnk
thnk
thnk
BOO
EVEN WITH THE FOUR OF US ATTACKING TOGETHER...
...TAPU LELE IS EASILY BRUSHING US ASIDE!
IT'S SO POWERFUL!
IF TAPU LELE IS THIS STRONG, HOW STRONG MUST THAT POKÉMON FROM ANOTHER WORLD BE TO HAVE DEFEATED IT?!
GOOD POINT...
IF WE HAVE TO FACE THAT POKÉMON IN THE FUTURE, WE'LL BE HELPLESS AGAINST IT!

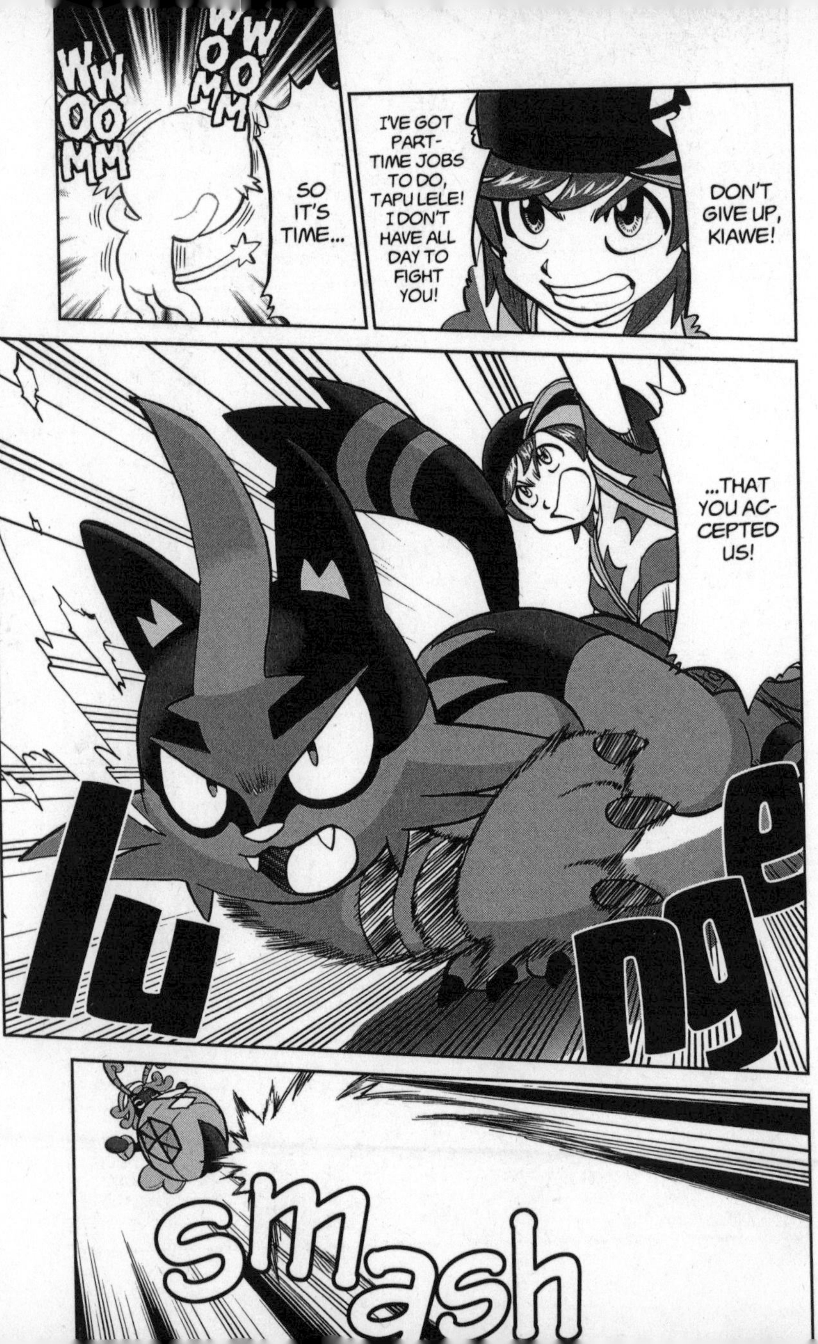
DON'T GIVE UP, KIAWE!
I'VE GOT PART-TIME JOBS TO DO, TAPU LELE! I DON'T HAVE ALL DAY TO FIGHT YOU!
WWOOMM
SO IT'S TIME...
WWOOMM
...THAT YOU ACCEPTED US!
lunge
smash

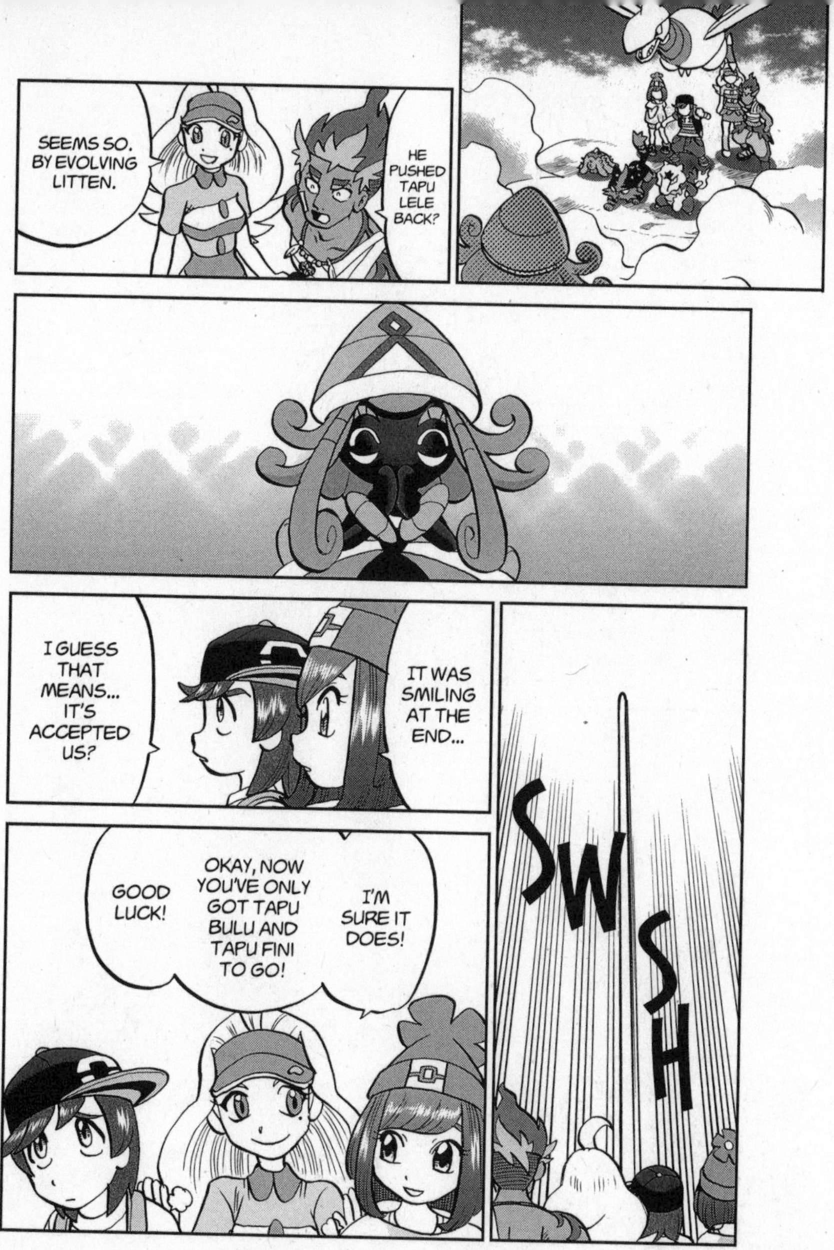
HE PUSHED TAPU LELE BACK?
SEEMS SO. BY EVOLVING LITTEN.
SWSH
IT WAS SMILING AT THE END...
I GUESS THAT MEANS... IT'S ACCEPTED US?
I'M SURE IT DOES!
OKAY, NOW YOU'VE ONLY GOT TAPU BULU AND TAPU FINI TO GO!
GOOD LUCK!

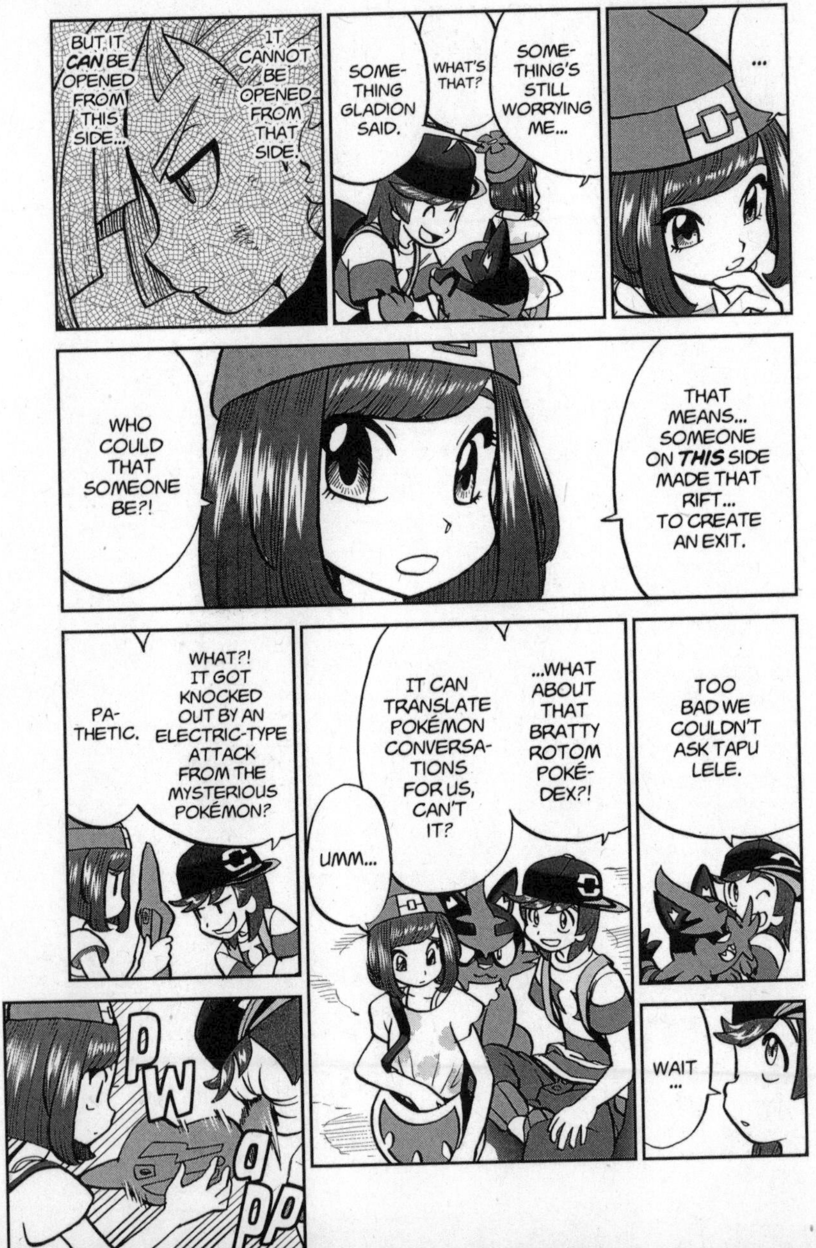
...
SOMETHING'S STILL WORRYING ME...
WHAT'S THAT?
SOMETHING GLADION SAID.
IT CANNOT BE OPENED FROM THAT SIDE.
BUT IT **CAN** BE OPENED FROM THIS SIDE...
THAT MEANS... SOMEONE ON **THIS** SIDE MADE THAT RIFT... TO CREATE AN EXIT.
WHO COULD THAT SOMEONE BE?!
TOO BAD WE COULDN'T ASK TAPU LELE.
WAIT...
...WHAT ABOUT THAT BRATTY ROTOM POKÉDEX?!
IT CAN TRANSLATE POKÉMON CONVERSATIONS FOR US, CAN'T IT?
UMM...
WHAT?! IT GOT KNOCKED OUT BY AN ELECTRIC-TYPE ATTACK FROM THE MYSTERIOUS POKÉMON?
PATHETIC.
PWOPP

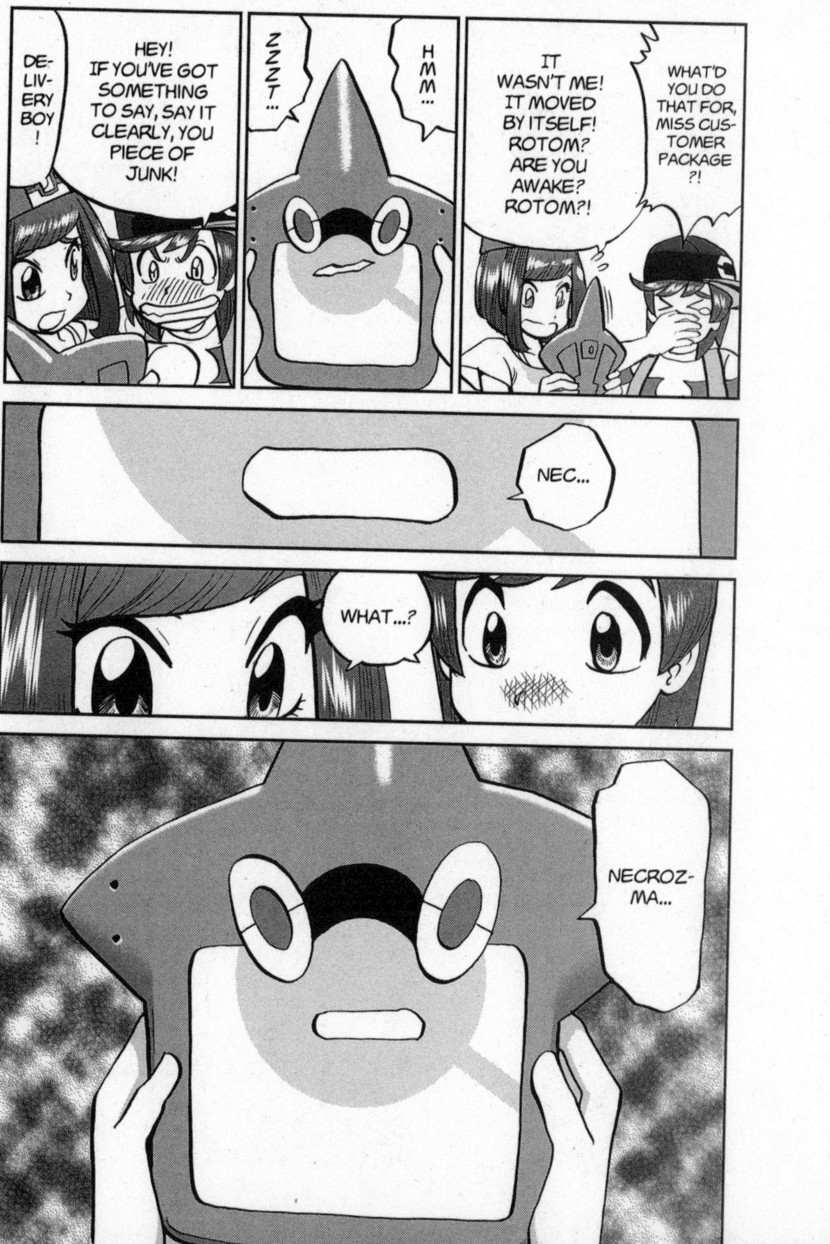
WHAT'D YOU DO THAT FOR, MISS CUSTOMER PACKAGE?!
IT WASN'T ME! IT MOVED BY ITSELF! ROTOM? ARE YOU AWAKE? ROTOM?!
HMM...
ZZZT...
HEY! IF YOU'VE GOT SOMETHING TO SAY, SAY IT CLEARLY, YOU PIECE OF JUNK!
DELIVERY BOY!
NEC...
WHAT...?
NECROZMA...

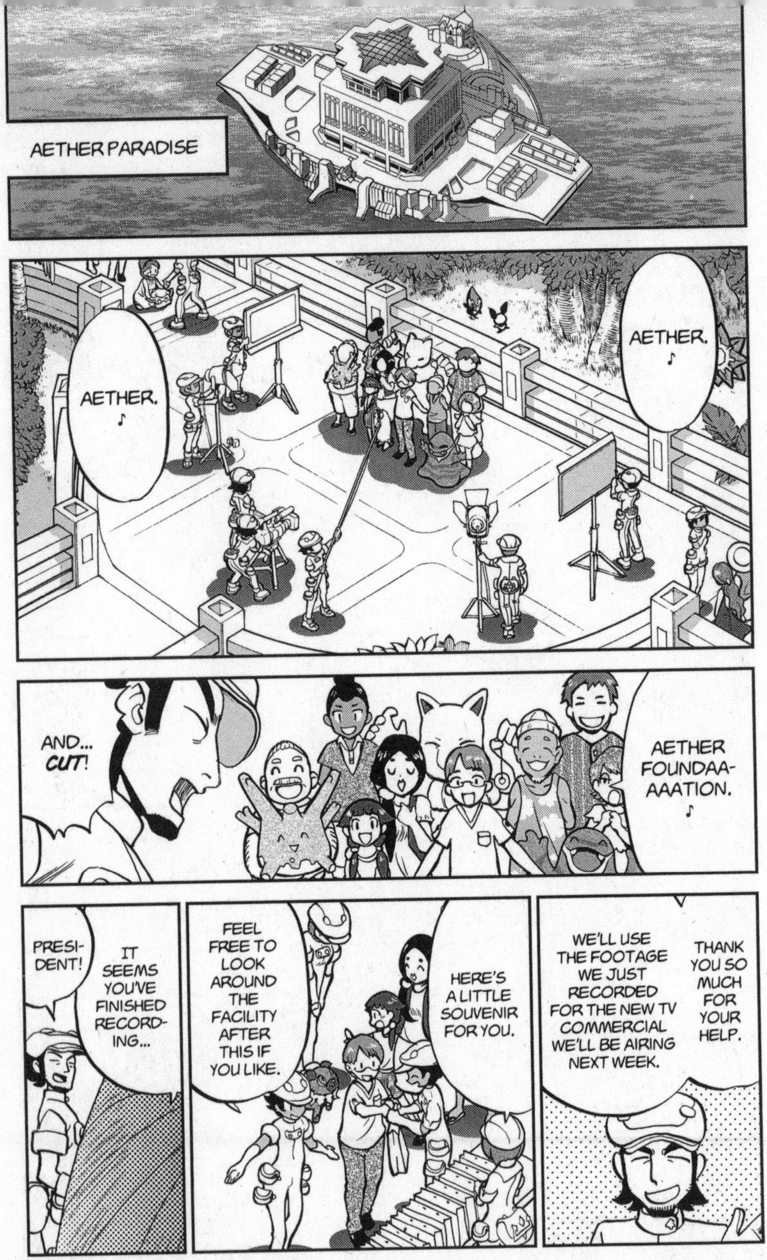
AETHER PARADISE
AETHER. ♪
AETHER. ♪
AETHER FOUNDAA-AAATION. ♪
AND... CUT!
THANK YOU SO MUCH FOR YOUR HELP.
WE'LL USE THE FOOTAGE WE JUST RECORDED FOR THE NEW TV COMMERCIAL WE'LL BE AIRING NEXT WEEK.
HERE'S A LITTLE SOUVENIR FOR YOU.
FEEL FREE TO LOOK AROUND THE FACILITY AFTER THIS IF YOU LIKE.
IT SEEMS YOU'VE FINISHED RECORDING...
PRESIDENT!

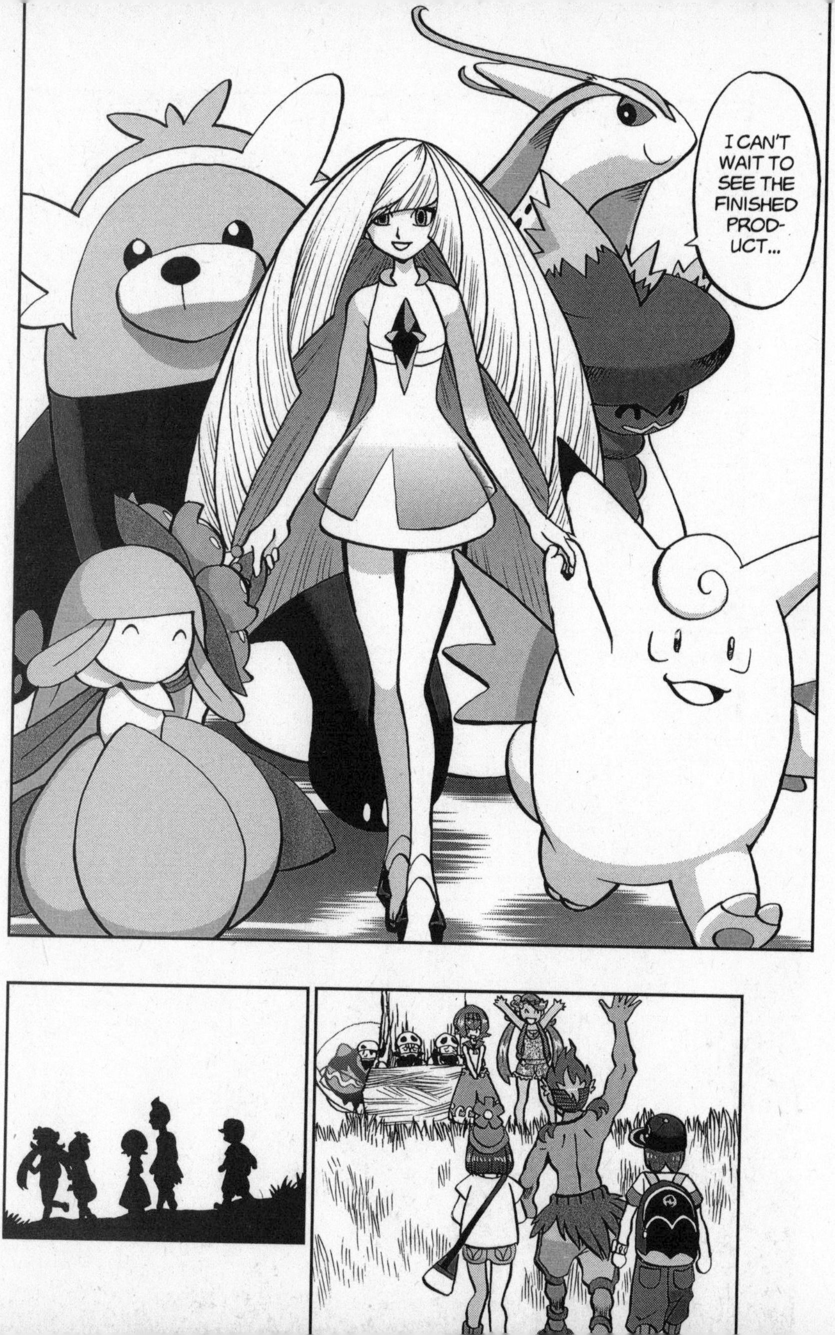
I CAN'T WAIT TO SEE THE FINISHED PROD-UCT...

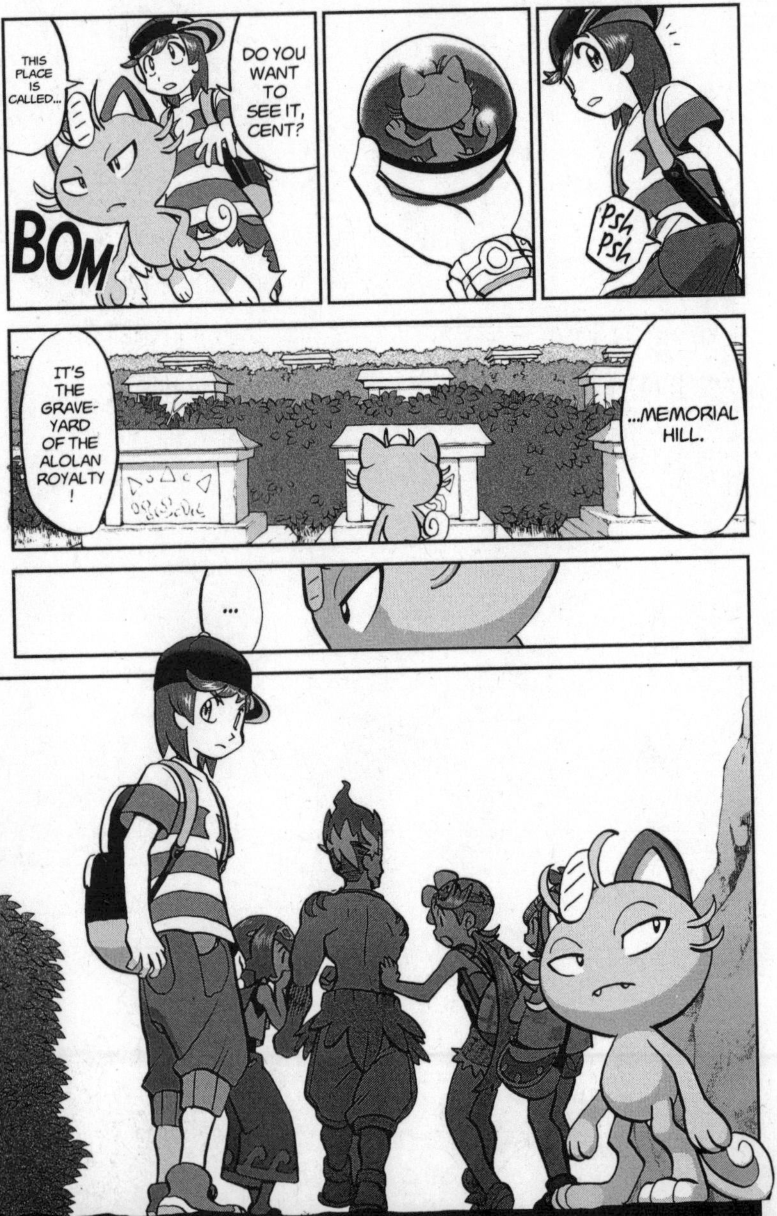
Psh Psh
DO YOU WANT TO SEE IT, CENT?
THIS PLACE IS CALLED...
BOM
...MEMORIAL HILL.
IT'S THE GRAVEYARD OF THE ALOLAN ROYALTY!
...

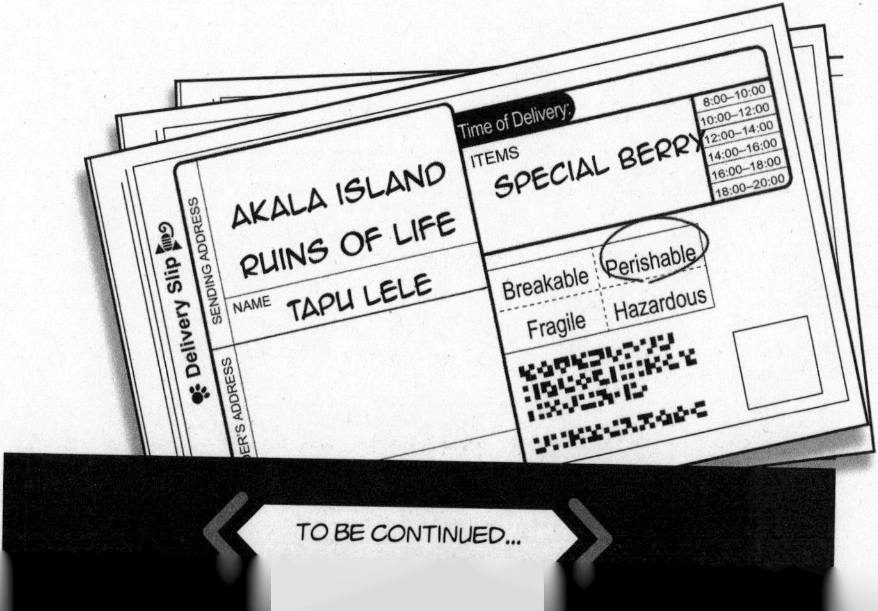
Delivery Slip
SENDING ADDRESS
AKALA ISLAND
RUINS OF LIFE
NAME
TAPU LELE
Time of Delivery:
ITEMS
SPECIAL BERRY
8:00–10:00
10:00–12:00
12:00–14:00
14:00–16:00
16:00–18:00
18:00–20:00
Breakable
Perishable
Fragile
Hazardous
TO BE CONTINUED...

Pokémon Sun & Moon
Volume 4
VIZ Media Edition

Story by HIDENORI KUSAKA
Art by SATOSHI YAMAMOTO

©2019 The Pokémon Company International.
©1995–2018 Nintendo / Creatures Inc. / GAME FREAK inc.
TM, ®, and character names are trademarks of Nintendo.
POCKET MONSTERS SPECIAL SUN • MOON Vol. 2
by Hidenori KUSAKA, Satoshi YAMAMOTO
© 2017 Hidenori KUSAKA, Satoshi YAMAMOTO
All rights reserved.
Original Japanese edition published by SHOGAKUKAN.
English translation rights in the United States of America, Canada, the United Kingdom,
Ireland, Australia, New Zealand and India arranged with SHOGAKUKAN.

Original Cover Design—Hiroyuki KAWASOME (grafio)

English Adaptation—Bryant Turnage
Translation—Tetsuichiro Miyaki
Touch-Up & Lettering—Susan Daigle-Leach
Design—Alice Lewis
Editor—Annette Roman

Printed in the U.S.A.

Published by
VIZ Media, LLC
P.O. Box 77010
San Francisco, CA 94107

10 9 8 7 6 5 4 3 2
First printing, May 2019
Second printing, September 2019

viz.com

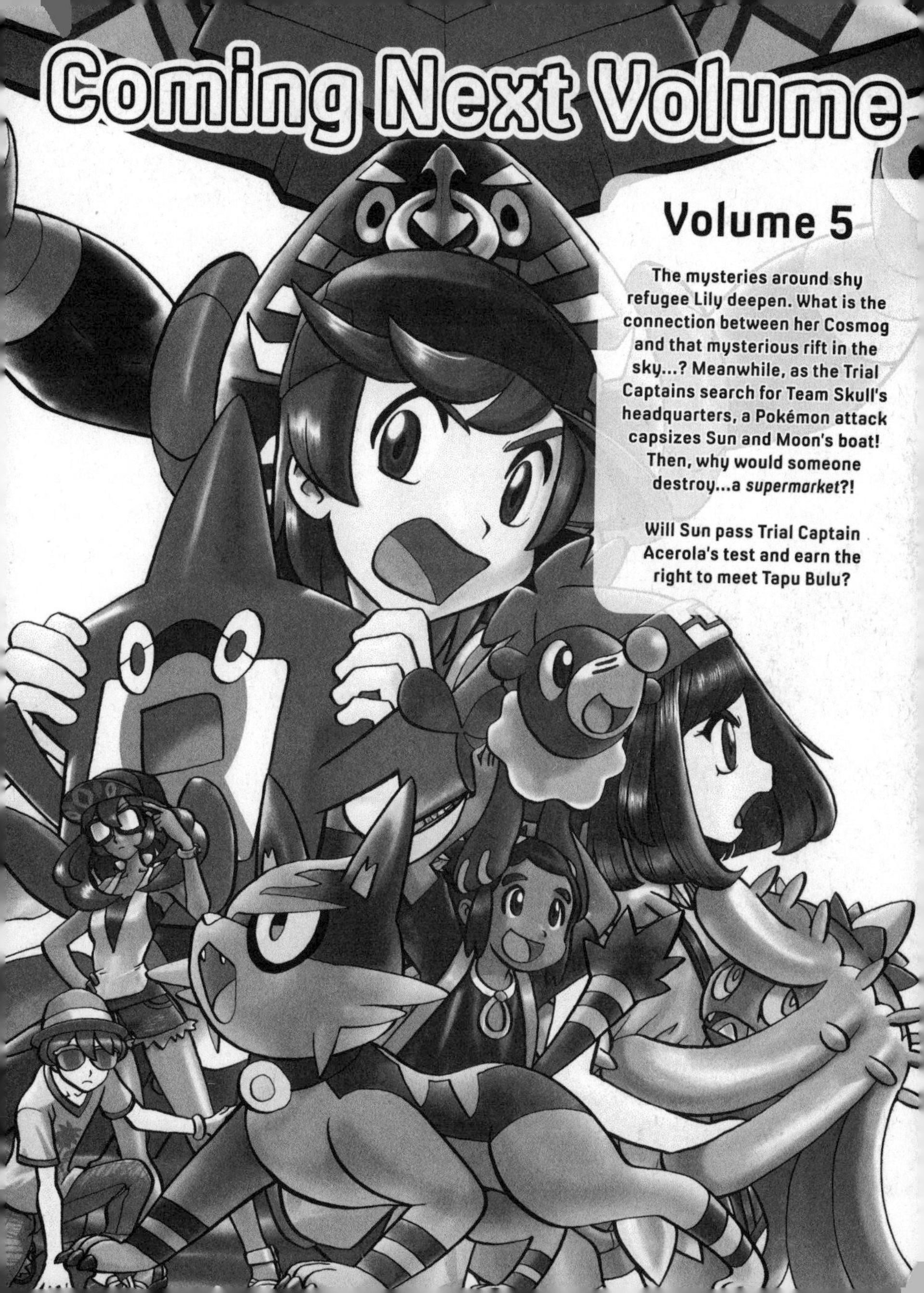
Coming Next Volume
Volume 5
The mysteries around shy refugee Lily deepen. What is the connection between her Cosmog and that mysterious rift in the sky...? Meanwhile, as the Trial Captains search for Team Skull's headquarters, a Pokémon attack capsizes Sun and Moon's boat! Then, why would someone destroy...a *supermarket*?!
Will Sun pass Trial Captain Acerola's test and earn the right to meet Tapu Bulu?

P9-DNY-324

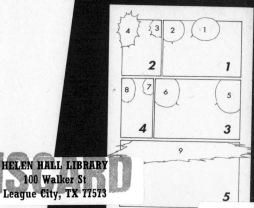

THIS IS THE END OF THIS GRAPHIC NOVEL!

To properly enjoy this VIZ Media graphic novel, please turn it around and begin reading from right to left.

This book has been printed in the original Japanese format in order to preserve the orientation of the original artwork. Have fun with it!

‹‹‹ READ THIS WAY!

Follow the action   May 21